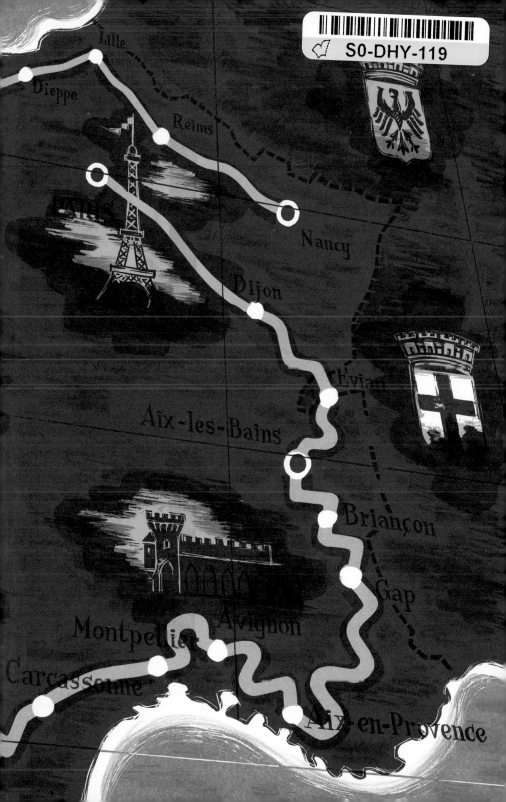

Oak Park Junior High,
November 25th, 1955.

Presented to Edward Radke

in recognition of his fine character,
high standard of academic achievement,
and special contribution to class 7A

for the year 1954-55.

THE BIG LOOP

Also by Claire Huchet Bishop

ALL ALONE

TWENTY AND TEN

BLUE SPRING FARM

PANCAKES-PARIS

AUGUSTUS

THE MAN WHO LOST HIS HEAD

THE BIG LOOP

by Claire Huchet Bishop

ILLUSTRATED BY

Carles Fontseré

The Viking Press

NEW YORK

1955

To

generous Gaston Riby

in memory of

our

Mouffetard Street

Contents

THE BIG LOOP

I. Surprise

"Show it to us! Show it to us, André!" shouted a group of twelve- and thirteen-year-old boys surrounding a frail, dark-haired boy, and pushing one another to get closer.

"Just a minute! Just a minute! Move back a little, all of you, so that I—"

"Back! Back!" gaily called Jack, a sturdy, redheaded boy, waving his arms like windmills toward the group. "Back! It's going to jump on us!"

A smile broke through on André's serious face. He said, "I mean that when you are all so near I can't even open my schoolbag."

"Don't listen to him!" barked a big blond boy whose name was Fernand. "He just hasn't got it—that's all. He's making it up."

"I am not! I am not!" André retorted hotly. "I *have* got it. It came in the mail this morning. Come over by the wall, all of you, and I'll show you."

They ran to the wall that enclosed the French boys' schoolyard. André steadied himself against the wall. He rested his schoolbag on his raised knee, and, folding back the flap, he bent his face and tried to pull something out with his right hand. All eyes were on that hand. Letting his schoolbag slide down at his feet, André straightened up and held out a photograph.

"Oh!" exclaimed all the boys with bated breath, and, all around, hands shot out to grab the picture. Quick as a flash, André stooped and dropped the photograph safely back into his schoolbag. There was a loud protest. "We didn't have time to see it! It's not fair!"

"Please!" begged curly-headed, chubby Michel. "Please, André! One more little peep—just one. To make sure it really is Bobet."

"It's Bobet, all right. No mistake," said Jack firmly.

There was a silence, full of envy and admiration. Bobet, the famous bicycle-racer, who was running the big race of the *Tour de France!*

Michel, who was nearsighted, asked, "Did he write anything on that picture, André?"

"Yep. 'To André Girard, future bicycle-racer. Cordially, L. Bobet.' "

Hardly had André finished quoting the sentence when Fernand broke into a loud guffaw. " 'Future bicycle-racer'! Little André! That's a good one! Surely Bobet never laid eyes on you, my pet. Have a look at yourself. 'Future bicycle-racer'! Ha, ha, ha!"

André reddened with anger. Ever since he had started to go to school, six years ago, Fernand had teased him and made his life miserable in one way or another. Sometimes André felt as if he could not stand it any longer, this continuous bullying and name-calling. And yet he never cringed under Fernand's meanness; he swallowed his tears and stood his ground and kept thinking, Someday, someday . . .

And now, while the nasty ha-ha's of Fernand were still ringing, André put his schoolbag hastily behind him and, hands in his pockets, head high, shouted, "What of it if I am not as big as you are! But you are nearly fourteen, and I will be thirteen next month."

"Oh yeah," drawled Fernand, addressing the crowd. "Little André thinks that within a few months he'll have calves like mine!" Triumphantly he slapped his hard, powerful legs. "It gives me a bellyache just to look at you, little André! Poor shriveled shrimp!"

Fists doubled, André rushed at Fernand, but Michel grabbed André's arm and stopped him midway, saying mildly, "Watch your schoolbag, André. And you, Fernand—after all, it is not always the strong-legged ones who win the *Tour de France*."

"Maybe it's boys like you, bookworm," mocked Fernand.

But Michel did not seem to hear him, though he turned a little pale as he said to André, "How did you do it—I mean, get the picture?"

"I wrote to Bobet."

"But that costs money—a fifteen-franc stamp."

"It's easy!" challenged Fernand. "Little André lifted it from his mother's purse!"

"I did not, I did not!" André yelled indignantly. "I saved a little at a time, last winter."

"Lugging coal from the cellar up to your fifth-floor neighbor, I bet," said Michel knowingly.

"How did you guess?"

"I just keep my eyes peeled."

"Lugging coal a whole winter—for fifteen francs!" Fernand spat. "Little André must think he's going to pedal with his arms!"

Laughter burst out here and there, and Fernand puffed out his chest, but Jack stepped quickly in front of him and said merrily, "Maybe *you've* won the *Tour* already, and nobody knows anything about it!"

And now a roar of laughter shook the whole group. Fernand's face darkened. There was no question that his game was being spoiled.

But as he did not relish a fight with someone as near his own age and as muscular as Jack, Fernand took his time to answer, and when he did he was slow and calculating. "Maybe *you* think *you* will win the *Tour* someday. But you won't. It takes money to train. Lots of it." He spat again and taunted, "And you haven't got any!"

"So what?" Jack cried gaily, turning his pants pockets inside out and dancing around wildly. "So what? I've got no money! Good! I'll be that much lighter on my bike!"

Again applause and laughter broke out on all sides, and Fernand muttered under his breath, "I'll get even with you someday, Mr. Joker!" Then he said grandly, "What's all the fuss about, anyhow? Little André has a picture of Bobet. Well, what of it? There are plenty of Bobet's mug around."

"Yes, my treasure," agreed Michel smoothly, "but not autographed and dedicated, you've got to admit that."

"Okay. What next? All of you are acting like a bunch of lunatics because of that picture—just as if Bobet were going to win the *Tour* this year."

"He is, he is!" shouted André.

"That's what you wish, because he is a Breton like you, little André. But he won't. Schaer has got a furious push at the sprint."

"But Bobet has a grip and a will!" cried André defiantly. "And he is a climber. Watch him in the Pyrenees mountain passes. I'd like to see your Schaer in the Tourmalet at six thousand feet!"

"Schaer!"

"Bobet!"

"No, Schaer!"

"No, Bobet!"

All the boys took sides, shouting at one another.

The schoolbell rang.

There were only ten days left until school closed, on

the thirteenth of July, yet everybody had to study just as hard as if it were the beginning of the term. School was like that. Nothing was ever accepted as an excuse: neither sickness nor outside circumstances. And as far as the big national annual sports event, the bicycle road race, the *Tour de France,* was concerned, the Parisian children were out of luck—the *Tour* ended in Paris on a Sunday, so they did not have the chance to be let out for a few hours on a weekday to see the cyclists go by, as did the country boys and girls.

As the boys stood in the classroom, near their desks, arms crossed on their chests, their minds were on the racers and not, of all things, on the coming arithmetic lesson.

Mr. Valeur, their teacher, looked at them and snapped his ruler down on his desk. They sat down in silence.

"Take out your arithmetic notebooks," said Mr. Valeur quietly.

What a bore! Problems, to be sure!

They spread their notebooks on their desks and waited for Mr. Valeur to speak. André, who had the tip of his pen in his mouth, wondered whether Mr. Valeur was interested in the *Tour* at all. No, he decided, the teacher could not be. He was too old. Probably forty. André imagined bespectacled Mr. Valeur in shorts, T-shirt, and sneakers, doubled up over the handlebars of a racing bicycle. He smiled.

Just then Mr. Valeur called, "Boys! Write: The front

wheel of a racing bicycle . . ." The whole class looked up sharply. Mr. Valeur did not seem to notice, as he repeated slowly, "The front wheel of a racing bicycle is twenty-four inches in diameter. The drive sprocket has forty-eight teeth, and the rear-wheel sprocket has twenty teeth. How far forward will the racer go with each revolution of the pedals?"

But this was not arithmetic any more! This was about the beloved contraption all French boys dream about—the bicycle, the *vélo,* or, more fondly, the Little Queen. Eagerly they jotted the figures down, and long before the end of the allotted time they started to get fidgety.

Mr. Valeur looked over his glasses at them. "Finished? All of you? Good! Girard, come to the blackboard."

Already André was at the front of the room, chalk in hand, and behind him the whole class, keenly alert, followed his writing.

A Diameter 24 in.
B Number teeth drive sprocket 48
C Number teeth rear-wheel sprocket 20

$$\frac{A\pi B}{C} \text{ or } \frac{24 \times 3.1416 \times 48}{20} = 180 \text{ in.} = 15 \text{ feet}$$

"Correct," approved Mr. Valeur. "Raise your hand, all of you who have this answer." Most of the pupils did.

Mr. Valeur made no comment, and, as soon as André was back at his place, he launched at once into the next problem. "A bicycle-racer leaves Paris for Le Havre at six a.m. His speed is eighteen miles an hour. Another racer also leaves Paris for Le Havre, at six-thirty. His speed is twenty-four miles an hour. The distance between Paris and Le Havre is one hundred and forty-five miles. How far from Le Havre will the second racer catch up with the first, and at what time?"

André raised his hand. "Please, sir—that is, providing there is no mishap on the road, isn't it? That they just go steadily?"

"Of course. This is a sort of ideal setup, you might say, not a regular time-trial race," answered Mr. Valeur.

The class groaned. Time-trial race! Old Valeur even knew about them! They were tense as the teacher continued. "In the time-trial race— By the way, are there many time-trial races in the *Tour de France?*"

"No!" the class yelled.

"Right. Only one or two in the whole *Tour,* because it is an endurance race, you might say. That and the mountain passes make or break the champions. Well, as I was saying, in a time-trial race, the racers are spaced in such a way around the clock, and they are all of such nearly equal strength, that they do not overtake one another, as they are supposed to do in that problem we have now. So, in actual time-trial racing, how do they know who is the winner? Renout?"

Jack jumped to his feet. "They never know, sir, until the last racer comes in and the timekeeper tells them."

"Correct. The last one in might have won, in fact. He might have made better time. Well, of course our present problem deals only with a made-up race for arithmetic purposes. So now, boys, find the answer."

Again they worked like mad for a few minutes, until Mr. Valeur called, "Fausset, what is the answer?"

"The second racer will catch up with the first racer one hundred and nine miles from Le Havre, and it will be eight o'clock."

"Right. Who else has that answer? Raise your hand!"

Four-fifths of the class did. There were always about ten boys out of the sixty-five who never made the grade in anything. But the school requirements were too exacting for Mr. Valeur to take extra time to give them special attention, no matter how much he wanted to do so. He could only watch to see that the usually good pupils did not slip into this unfortunate category. So when he saw that Jack, who was an average student, had not raised his hand, he inquired, "Renout, what was your answer to the problem?"

"I did not get any, sir."

"You mean you could not even begin to try to figure it out?"

"No, sir, I could not."

"But why?" insisted Mr. Valeur. "What was wrong?"

Jack cleared his throat and opened his eyes wide. " 'Cause the guy, I mean the second racer, he never got started. He had a flat tire."

The class roared with laughter. Mr. Valeur brought his ruler down on his desk sharply. The class stopped at once and waited in awe for the teacher's next words. Jack had answered him with a joke! In the classroom! What would his punishment be?

Mr. Valeur said very quietly, "I am surprised at you, Renout. I thought you knew a lot about the *Tour*."

"But, s-sir—" stammered Jack, surprised.

"Do not interrupt, please. Your second racer, who, you say, got a flat tire, apparently sat down in a ditch and gave up."

Jack was very red. "Sir—sir—" he repeated, and he started sliding down to his seat.

"Please remain standing," commanded Mr. Valeur. "Can anyone tell Renout what his second racer should have done?"

"Repair!" yelled the class.

"Of course. And would that delay him long, Girard?"

"No, sir. Some racers can make repairs in less than fifty seconds."

Mr. Valeur arched his eyebrows. "Are you sure, Girard? Remove the casing, find the leak in the tube, patch it, put the whole thing back? Maybe he carries a whole new inner tube, and he does not have to patch—is that it? But, just the same, fifty seconds!"

Jack begged, "Sir—sir—please!"

Mr. Valeur ignored him and motioned to André, who hated to answer, because of Jack. "He does not have to do all that, sir. That was in the old days. Now racing bicycles have tubeless tires, all in one piece. They are much lighter, and repairing goes faster. You just pry the whole

tire off the rim and put on another tire and make it stick
with cement."

"Right," approved Mr. Valeur. "But apparently our
friend Renout's racer did not have any spare tubeless
tires. We all know that this is very strange, since all racers carry tires around their shoulders. But this particular
racer was completely out of luck, was he not, Renout?"

"Well, sir," said Jack, who was both eager and embarrassed, "not exactly. Because there are always mechanics
around in a race. And also, anyone on the racer's team
could just hand over his own bike. In a race the motto is
solidarity."

Mr. Valeur looked over his glasses at Jack, and there
was a small twinkle in his eyes as he said, "Right. So,
Renout, would you say that your second racer had no excuse for not starting?"

"Yes, sir. He had no excuse."

"All right. Then you catch up with him tonight at

home, please, and bring me the correct answer tomorrow, neatly written in your notebook. Now sit down, Renout. And since we are talking of tubeless tires, does any one of you boys know that there was a time when bicycles did not have even ordinary tires with casings and tubes? Way back, there was nothing at all, just a wooden circle. Then later there was a solid strip of plain rubber. You can imagine how rough it was to ride on such a thing! Of course, racing contests were impossible. In fact, very few people used bicycles. But children loved them. And so it happened that in 1888 there was a man in Ireland— Fausset, go to the map and show us Ireland—no, no, not Newfoundland, my boy! Ireland! Over there, west of England. Yes.

"Well, there in Ireland lived a man, an animal doctor, a veterinary, whose name was John Boyd Dunlop—"

"Dunlop tires!" yelled André.

"You should have raised your hand, Girard," said Mr. Valeur gently. "However, since it is the end of the year we will let it go. Yes, Dunlop tires—and this is the story that is told. Mr. Dunlop had a son, who had a tricycle, which, of course, had those plain, solid rubber strips on the wheels. Young John Dunlop complained all the time, saying, 'Daddy, can't you do something? It's awfully hard riding on this and bouncing all the time!' One day, just as his father had finished operating on an animal and was removing his rubber gloves, young John came in and complained again about his tricycle. At that moment the rubber gloves stuck, and Mr. Dunlop did what everybody does when this happens: he put the glove to his lips and blew, and the glove puffed up. And, as it did, Mr. Dunlop got the tire idea! He himself related later how he at once got hold of some rubber and some sort of glue and started working; and how after many trials and errors he finally succeeded in making a long, hollow tube into which he pumped some air with his son's football pump and closed it with a baby-bottle nipple. Then he called for young Dunlop to try the new gadget."

Mr. Valeur opened a book called *Le Cyclisme*, by Raymond Hutier, and said, "This is what Mr. Dunlop wrote about this memorable event:

"The sun had set when my son John, for the first time, sat astride his strange machine. I remember everything very distinctly: there was an eclipse of the moon that day and I can still recall my son's happy face in the pale light.

"So the tire was born! Mr. Dunlop's idea of a rubber tube full of air proved so successful that it was used not only for bicycles, but also for automobiles, later."

Fernand raised his hand. "Did Mr. Dunlop make a lot of money?"

"Well, I suppose so, although inventors don't get rich necessarily. But probably Mr. Dunlop did. However, the big thrill was not in moneymaking but in finding out, inventing, the pneumatic rubber tire. That made all sorts of things possible. Bicycle-racing, for instance. How many of you would like to become professional racers?"

There were many hands raised, among them André's, Jack's, Michel's, and Fernand's.

Mr. Valeur smiled and inquired, "And how many of you want to make a lot of money?"

Fernand raised his hand.

"But Fausset," exclaimed Mr. Valeur, "you already raised your hand before, for professional racing!"

"Sir," said Fernand sharply, "I want to be a professional racer and get rich *too*."

The other pupils said, "Oh!" They were shocked.

Fernand snapped back belligerently, "There is money in bicycle-racing. Big prizes. Engagements on the tracks. That's why I want to go in for it. For the money."

"Well," said Mr. Valeur evenly, "I hope you won't be disappointed when you get rich, if ever you do. You would be surprised how few rich people are happy. But to come back to our first arithmetic problem about sprockets—do you know, all of you, that there was a time when not only were there no sprockets, but there was not even a single chain to help propel the bicycle?"

"No chain!" The boys gasped.

"No," went on Mr. Valeur. "At the beginning, in 1779, the bicycle that was presented to Louis the Sixteenth at the court of Versailles was only a two-wheel affair linked together by a horizontal wooden bar. In 1816 Mr. Niepce, who is also known for his work in photography, improved the bicycle, making it a sort of hobbyhorse; the rider sat on the horizontal bar, which ended in a carved animal's head, and propelled himself with his feet.

"In 1861 there was a man in Paris by the name of Pierre Michaux who was a mechanic. Mr. Michaux had a son. He also had a neighbor who was a gentlemen's hat-maker and owned a celeripede, as the bicycle was called then. This hatmaker brought his celeripede to Mr. Michaux for repairs, and went back to his hatmaking. After Mr. Michaux had repaired it, he said to his son, 'Take it around the block and see if it is all right.' The boy was delighted. He went around the block, and then, as the Avenue Montaigne was slightly hilly, he went down fast and of course did not have to use his legs at all. When he came back, he said to his father, 'It works all right, Papa. But isn't it too bad that one cannot use one's legs when going downhill? The legs are useless.'

" 'The legs are useless.' This gave Mr. Michaux and his employee, a man named Pierre Lallemant, an idea. They put a piece of metal through the hub of the front wheel, and two spools—like spools for thread—at the two ends of the piece of metal. The legs of the rider did not have to trail on the ground any more. He could rest them on the spools, which, at the same time, he could make revolve around the central axis, and thereby propel the bicycle. Michaux's store, Twenty-nine Avenue Montaigne in Paris, was the first store in the world where bicycles were made and sold commercially. In those days they sold for two hundred francs apiece, which was very expensive at the time. Later Pierre Lallemant emigrated to the United States; and there he made the same kind of bicycles. The Americans called them 'boneshakers.' "

The class had a good laugh. All the pupils were amazed to hear that because two boys—young Michaux and young Dunlop—had spoken up, rotary cranks and pneumatic tires had been invented! They all listened eagerly to what Mr. Valeur had to say next about the bicycle.

"In due time," he continued, "the chain was invented. You might say it was like a flexible metal thread connecting the revolving back spool and the pedals. And later something else was invented which played an important part in the history of bicycle-racing. Who can tell me what it is? Mayer?"

"The gear shift, sir," said Michel.

"Aren't you going a little too fast?"

"Well, sir, before the gear shift was invented, if the racer wanted to change gears he had to get off, remove his rear wheel, and reverse its position. With the gear shift he can change gears while riding."

"Correct. So, first came the possibility of changing gears by having two sprockets with different numbers of teeth. In order to use one or the other the racer had to reverse the position of his rear wheel. And then the gear shift was introduced. It is, relatively speaking, a newcomer. It was not widely in use until after World War One. When was that, Renout?"

"Nineteen-fourteen to nineteen-eighteen, sir."

"Right. The gear shift is used by racers of all nationalities, and they call it by its French name, *dérailleur*, though of course they do not pronounce it the way a French person does. But anyway, it is still a gear shift, that wonderful simple gadget that enables a cyclist to

change gears without stepping off his bike. A gear shift
looks something like this." Mr. Valeur went to the blackboard.

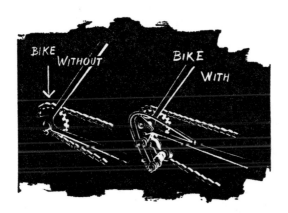

"And now, Renout, suppose you want to climb a hill—
will you set your gear shift for a low or high gear? That's
a mathematical problem."

"For a low gear, sir."

"Why?"

"Because in a low gear I'll move my feet faster and with
less effort, and that will help me go uphill."

"Correct. And now, Fausset, how would you run on
level ground?"

"In a high gear, sir."

"Why, Girard?"

"Because I would cover more ground each time I made
a complete revolution of the pedals."

"Correct. What other reason, Renout?"

"Because that way I would not get so tired." He grinned happily.

"Well," said Mr. Valeur, who could not help smiling too, "for once you hit it right with your joke, Renout. Now, who can tell me how a gear works—a high gear, for instance? Mayer?"

"In a high gear there is a big difference between the number of teeth in the drive sprocket and the number of teeth in the rear-wheel sprocket."

"Very good. You don't have a bicycle, Mayer, do you?"

"No, sir."

"And you, Girard?"

"No, sir."

"And you, Fausset?"

"No, sir, but—"

"And you, Renout?"

"No, sir."

"Has anyone in the class?"

No one raised a hand, and Mr. Valeur commented, "I thought so. Yet you all know a great deal about bicycles. You probably hang around bicycle stores and people who have bicycles. I used to do the same when I was your age. I had just passed thirteen when I had my first bike, a sports model—no gear shift, of course. From then on I started training. Every day. I was fifteen when I entered small amateur contests. I raced Paris to Rambouillet, Paris to Chantilly. Why, I even raced Paris to Brest, and I won!"

At first the boys were so surprised that they sat in

silence. Then they burst into a thunder of applause. Old, dignified Valeur winning a bicycle race, even if it had been an amateur one! And André had thought of making fun of him dressed as a racer! But this was marvelous news, even if it had happened so long ago! It made them all feel that Mr. Valeur was one of them. They were so happy that they wanted to laugh and shout.

Mr. Valeur said gently, "Quiet, boys. There is no reason to run wild simply because I won a bicycle race —in the Dark Ages. Anyway, it was just a small semi-professional race— nothing like training for the Big Loop!"

They gasped. The Big Loop! He even knew that popular expression!

"By the way, why is it called the Big Loop? Mayer?"

"Because the racers go all around France, and the circuit is like a big loop."

"Yes, and the Big Loop is the greatest annual outdoor sports event in France—something like the World Series in America. And speaking of America, why is there no bicycle *Tour* there? Girard?"

"Because America is too big. The racers would break down."

"That's right. Even France is quite a stretch to cover on a bicycle in twenty-one to twenty-five consecutive days. The Big Loop is about three thousand miles, depending on the itinerary. Do you know when this national contest started?"

The whole class shouted, "Nineteen-oh-three!"

"Yes. That's a long time ago, isn't it? And it all began with a man whose name you should know—Henri Desgranges. Few people had bicycles at that time, and still fewer, in France, knew anything about physical training of any sort. In addition, the roads were dirt roads, full of holes and ruts. But Desgranges saw ahead. He was a man with vision. He was a pioneer."

"He was a poet," whispered Michel.

Mr. Valeur stopped and looked at Michel thoughtfully, apparently forgetting that Michel had not raised his hand. Then he said, "I never thought of him that way, But I guess you are right, Mayer. Not only did he love the contraption itself—the bicycle—but he loved the exhilarating sense of freedom that a man feels through traveling under his own power. The call of the road, answered through one's own muscular effort, applied to a simple machine. Yes, Henri Desgranges probably never wrote a line of poetry, but, indeed, he was a poet."

The bell rang. How short school had seemed that afternoon! Mr. Valeur said, "We talked so much that I did not have time to explain to you in detail about your geography assignment for tomorrow. At home, look in your geography textbooks and find out all you can about the country covered by the racers today, from Strasbourg to Metz—how it looks; what kind of soil there is; the geological formation; rivers; mountains; what is grown in that region; the monuments; the historical spots. You may need your dictionaries and your history books to get all the information. And now, that's all for today. *Bonsoir, mes enfants."*

The boys stood up in silence and filed out, one row after another, bending their heads as they passed in front of Mr. Valeur, and saying, *"Bonsoir, M'sieu."* They went along the hall two by two, still without talking. Then the street at last—and wild shrieks, jumps, arms flinging schoolbags around.

Usually they dispersed pretty quickly, but today the sixth grade could not tear itself apart. Such an afternoon! If school were only like that all year round! And what a surprise! Who would have expected old Valeur to know so much about bicycles and racing—and to tell about it right in the classroom! Well, of course, it was true that he had always been pretty decent; he was strict, but he was fair. Yes, that's what they liked about him—he was fair. And now, in addition, he had been fun. Well, it made one feel downright sorry that school was almost over. And who had ever felt that way before?

But Fernand put a damper on his classmates' enthusiasm, saying, "Phew! Valeur had to quit racing because he was too puny—somewhat like little André!"

"I'll show you!" yelled André, trying to get away from Michel's grip.

"Come on," said Michel. "Come on! Leave him alone. Let's go."

Jack eyed Fernand from head to foot, and, shrugging his shoulders, said, "Pitiful! Just pitiful!"

"Pitiful yourself!" hissed Fernand. "Do you know the other reason why Valeur could not make the grade in racing? Because he was like you. No money. See?" He stuck out his tongue in Jack's direction.

"Oh, move on, Rockefeller!" Jack called back as he joined André and Michel, while laughter rang out in the group.

"Come on!" urged Michel again. And the three of them set out in the direction of Mouffetard Street.

II. A Plan

As the three friends shuffled along the Paris streets, trying to walk under the trees to avoid the hot July sun,
their minds were not on the coming vacation but on the
Tour, on the Big Loop—and on what Mr. Valeur had
said about it and about the bicycle.

Suddenly Jack stopped and slapped his forehead. "I
have an idea! André, why don't you show old Valeur your
picture of Bobet? The old guy deserves it. Who knows,
he might even make a pinup of it, for the whole class!
That would be something! What do you think?"

"Wonderful! But how am I going to sell the idea to old
V.? I can't talk to him while we are in line; that's not
allowed. And can you see me raising my hand in the

classroom and saying, 'Sir, I have a photograph I'd like to show you.' I could be sure of getting a bad mark and never have a chance to produce the picture. Right?"

"Leave it to me," said Michel with a wink. "I think I can fix it so old V. will be the one who will ask you about the picture. Only watch out: you must act awfully surprised when he does it."

"Check," agreed André. "I won't even ask you now what you have in mind, so that I will be surprised."

Jack rubbed his hands in glee. "Oh, boy! Won't you-know-who be mad if it works! I bet he'll have a fit!"

Michel lifted his finger in warning. "Watch out for him! He's a snake in the grass!"

"Takes a lot more to frighten me," said Jack cheerfully.

"He's just jealous," put in André.

"Jealous of what?" retorted Michel. "Don't you know that he's going to get a bike, a brand-new one, for the New Year?"

Jack and André stopped walking. "No!" they gasped. "How do you know?"

"He told me."

"Told *you?*"

"What's the matter? It's not forbidden to talk to Fernand, is it?"

"No, of course not," Jack admitted reluctantly.

"Just the same—" André burst out.

"Just the same, what?" asked Michel quietly. "If you don't talk to him, how are you going to find out what he's up to? Anyway, I didn't go after him. He came to me. He wanted to know how to spell 'bicycle,' 'handlebar,' and 'brakes.' "

"Well, of course." André nodded. "You are the best speller in the class. But why did he want to know?"

"That's just it. I wanted to know too. So I said, 'I'll tell you how to spell those words if you tell me first what for. And no fooling. If you fib, I'll find out.' He was furious, but he came across—he had to. He said he was writing his uncle, who had asked him what he wanted for a New Year present, and—"

"He was asking his uncle for a bicycle!" interrupted André. "Just like that—'Dear Uncle, send me a bike.' Can you beat it!"

Jack rolled his eyes and puffed out his cheeks. "I'll be darned! That's why he tried to slay me with his 'You haven't got any money.' His uncle—"

"Oh," Michel interrupted calmly, "after all, it doesn't take that much money to buy a bicycle. His uncle doesn't have to be a millionaire."

"No? Well," asked Jack, "then just tell me this—can *your* folks afford to buy you one?"

Michel bent his head as if to hide his face. "No, they can't. And if they could, they wouldn't anyway."

"Why?"

"Because—because— Because it might mean buying another one within two years or so, when I'm taller."

"Right," said Jack. "And I'll bet that Mrs. Girard can't afford to buy a bike either. Isn't that true, André?"

"Yes. My mother couldn't afford it now. She has been

saving for it, though, ever since I was ten years old. That's three years ago. I know. She told me. I think about it all the time. She said that maybe next year, if I graduate, it will be my graduation present."

"See?" Jack concluded. "And as far as I am concerned, I know darn well that with five of us in the family, plus Papa and Mama, there is not a single chance of my getting a bicycle until I buy it myself with my own hard-earned money. I'll go to work right after graduation and start saving. But Fernand—no one has to slave and save for his bicycle! He writes his uncle, and, zoom, he gets it! See what I mean? Oh well, who cares? I'll still make it!" Jack's face broke into a large carefree smile as he slapped his two friends on the shoulders.

"I will too!" echoed André, raising his head proudly.

"You bet!" added Michel quietly.

For a while they walked in silence. Suddenly they heard shouts. "Papers! Papers! Papers!" They glanced at one another and with one accord started to run toward the subway entrance.

"Papers! Get your paper! Latest news of the *Tour!* Night edition! Get your paper!" shouted the newsdealer, who was holding the pile in such a way that no one could read the headlines.

The three boys dashed in and out of the crowd, trying to catch a glimpse of the papers people had already bought. But it seemed that those who had papers were just as anxious as the newsdealer not to let anybody get a free glance. The boys were smart and patient, however, and at last a jovial-looking man stopped and spread his sheet in front of them.

"Want to see? Have a look. Schaer is ahead, Wagtmans close behind."

"Schaer is on the Swiss team, isn't he?" said Jack. "And Wagtmans on the Dutch team?"

"That's right."

"What about Bobet?" André asked anxiously.

"Nothing about him today, it seems. But don't worry, the French team, the Tricolores, still has plenty of time to win. Three weeks to go, you know. Three weeks to go," the man went on, talking now to a man he had never seen before as they stepped down the subway steps. Everybody was talking to everybody else about the *Tour*.

André, Jack, and Michel also weighed the situation. Jack said, "That man was right. It doesn't mean a thing to win one stretch of the *Tour*."

"No," said Michel. "You just get the prize money and the green sweater of the stretch winner."

"That's it," said Jack. "It doesn't mean that you're going to be the big winner of the whole *Tour*. Why, it might even happen that the one who wins the *Tour* never wins a single stretch."

"For instance," asked André, "could Bobet be far behind today and still win the *Tour?*"

"Of course," said Jack convincingly. "Don't you worry. That picture of yours in going to be worth a lot soon. Old V. had better show it to the whole class now, before it's no longer safe for you to air it!"

Michel sighed. "I wish I knew all about today's race. Even the evening papers cannot tell everything. I wish we had a radio."

"Wish we had one too," echoed André. "Fernand has one."

"That's a big help to the three of us!" Jack said, laughing. They all giggled.

"Say, Jack," remarked Michel, "I thought I'd die laughing when you told old V. that your cyclist of the problem had a flat tire! How did you ever think of such a thing?"

"Don't know. Just came out. It didn't turn out so well, though, did it? But how was I to expect that old V. would enter the game and kid me along? And now I've got to do that problem all over again tonight, and that's no joke, because it's the kind of problem I can never figure out anyway."

"Come home with me and I'll show you," André suggested.

"Great! But why not come to my place instead?"

"Okay. But first we must go and ask my mother."

"Is she home now?"

"Yes, her schedule this week at the post office is from eight to one and from six to eight."

"Ah," shouted Michel gaily, "here is my mother! Goodby! Don't forget, André—I'll fix it with old V. about Bobet's picture!"

Hastily he shook hands and ran toward a woman coming from the opposite direction. When he reached her they kissed each other affectionately. The woman waved to André and Jack and went away with Michel, who had taken her arm.

"He loves her just as much as if she were his own, real mother, doesn't he?" said André.

"Yep. And Mr. Morel too, as if he were not Michel's adopted father."

"I wonder if he remembers his own parents? He never talks about them. What do you think, Jack?"

" 'Course he remembers them! He was five years old when they were killed during the war. His whole family! It's ghastly to think of it. It was just luck that he escaped. Poor Michel! And he is so smart—and such a good friend! He always seems to me much older than we are."

"Maybe," said André, "when one suffers it makes one old."

They came to the street where they lived, Mouffetard Street—La Mouff', as it is called—one of the oldest streets in Paris; steep, crooked, with crumbling houses and narrow sidewalks crowded with food stands—a street always filled with noise and children. People who live there do not necessarily know one another, but in the street they talk together freely, and whatever happens on the sidewalk concerns everybody.

Just then André and Jack noticed people gathering and heard somebody screaming. They edged their way through the crowd, trying to see what the matter was. There stood the chestnut vendor, an elderly woman, holding a bedraggled cat in her arms and shouting at the top of her voice, "He will pay for it! He will, someday! Mark

my words! To do such a thing to a poor innocent cat! He
is a bandit, a gangster!"

"Who? What happened?" André and Jack asked the
people around them.

"Oh, big Fernand. He just came back from school and
he caught the old lady's cat and tied a tin can to its
tail . . . A disgrace . . . for our street . . . for his
parents. . . . It's all the fault of that rich uncle. . . .
The kid is being spoiled to death. . . . There is no man-
aging him any more. . . . It will end badly . . ."

André and Jack shrugged their shoulders knowingly.
Then they turned toward André's house. In the long, narrow, dark, damp hall, its stone walls shiny and smooth
from years of being rubbed by human bodies, André
went first and Jack followed. And then up, up, the rickety,
winding old wooden stairs. On the landings the boys held
their noses as they passed the toilets, one for each floor.
On the fourth floor André knocked at one of the three
doors. The door opened, and he was in his mother's arms.

"And here is Jack," he said.

André's mother shook hands and said, "Good. Come
in, both of you. You can have a snack."

"Well, Maman, it is just that we are going to do a little
work together, Jack and I, and—"

"Fine. You can eat first and then use the table."

"Thank you, but, Maman, I just came to say that, if it
is all right with you, we are going to Jack's house to
work."

Mrs. Girard's face clouded, but she caught herself and

said gently, "But you can have a snack before you go, can't you?"

They both nodded and said, "Thank you."

Mrs. Girard was happy again as they sat at the round table in the center of the room, which also contained a coal stove and a gas burner, a sink, a dresser, four chairs, an armchair, and a daybed. André had a tiny room to himself off the main room; it was just large enough for his bed and the old hand-hewn Breton oak wardrobe. He had to wash in the kitchen sink. His mother slept on the daybed in the living room. When she went to work early or came back late she could slip in and out of the apartment without waking André.

Now Maman cut big chunks from a long loaf of French bread, and then she broke a piece of chocolate in two. André looked at her. He lowered his head. Maman rested her eyes on him, hesitated an instant, then turned around and opened the dresser. Out came the jar of strawberry jam.

"Maman made it last summer!" André volunteered joyfully.

"Yes," said Maman. "I had a nice break on the strawberries, so even with the sugar it did not cost much, for a little treat once in a while."

"I'm crazy about strawberry jam," said Jack appreciatively.

Maman sat down with them. No, she would not eat anything now. She would have supper early, before going back to the post office.

They told her about the marvelous afternoon at school. Of course she knew about André's having received Bobet's picture. She sighed. "Yes, André takes after his father."

"My father was on the French team!" said André proudly.

"You don't say!" exclaimed Jack. "And you never told me all these years! Did he win?"

"No. He was injured."

"That was before we were married," Maman went on. "While he was training, a jealous yellow dog gave him a push and he fell down a mountain slope and was permanently disabled for racing."

"The French team always said he was the most promising racer they ever had!" put in André.

"Yes, they expected great things from him. He himself always felt he could have won the *Tour*," explained Maman.

"His son will!" said André forcefully, pointing to his chest.

"You bet!" Jack approved warmly.

Maman shook her head sadly. "To tell you the truth, I wish André would not talk that way. First of all, he does not have the physique for a racer. Now if he were a strapping young chap like you, Jack—"

"Maman!" cried André reproachfully.

"Well, I know you don't like my saying it, André, but it is the truth and you might as well face it."

"Oh, Madame, but you never can tell! Who knows? André might turn out to be—a giant."

Maman smiled. "Maybe. Anyway, André will have his bike for graduation if all goes well. He has his heart set on it, and I have promised. But it does not follow that he will be a racer. By the time I married my husband he had become a chef, but he still had his bike."

"He did have a bike?" queried Jack.

"Yes. I see what's on your mind, Jack. No, I don't have the bike any more. During the occupation it was taken by the Nazis when they caught my husband carrying secret messages for the Resistance."

Jack nodded gravely. He knew that André's father had been shot. Silently the three of them looked toward the dresser at the elaborately framed picture of a good-looking man. Next to it was another photograph, a colored photograph of a wedding. One could see that Mr. Girard was wearing his Sunday-best suit. Mrs. Girard was more difficult to recognize because she wore the lovely costume of her village in Brittany: a pert little white cap with streamers; upturned starched wings of spotless white linen on the shoulders; a tight black velvet bodice; a full black skirt with a large velvet border; and a beautiful little silk apron, hand embroidered all over with colored birds and flowers.

After the Girards had come to Paris, Maman did not wear her Breton costume any more, except once in a while, on special occasions—such as a ball of all the Bretons in

Paris, where they all wore the different costumes of their districts and spoke to each other in their difficult Gaelic language. But Maman had not worn her beautiful costume since before the war. It lay folded in mothballs in a big box above the wardrobe.

As if to dispel the gloom Maman asked, "What was all the noise in the streets about? Did you see?"

They told her. Maman said, "Poor Fernand!"

"Poor! He would not like that!" Jack laughed.

"Fernand is going to have a bike—a brand-new one. For the New Year," said André.

"No. Really?"

"Some people have all the luck—health and money. He will be able to start training long before I do," said Jack.

"But your father has a bike, hasn't he, Jack? He couldn't do without it, going back and forth from his street-digger's job."

"Yes, Madame, that's just it. It's for his work, so he nurses it like a baby. I can't even get near the contraption. Guess he's afraid that just a glance from me and it would fall apart!"

Maman laughed. "Well, indeed, I guess you had better stay away from that bike. But you don't have to stay away from the strawberry jam."

The boys helped themselves promptly.

"You know what?" Jack said. "In America, bread loaves are square."

"Square?" exclaimed André.

"Yep. A girl friend of my sister gave her an American magazine, and it shows a boy eating a square piece of bread."

"How funny!"

"Wait, it's even funnier: on that square piece of bread there is butter *and* jam—together."

"Together!" Both André and Maman gasped.

"Yes. Can you beat it? Maybe it's not true, though. Just an ad."

"Wish we knew an American He could tell us," said André.

"Maybe it is true," Maman commented slowly. "America is rich. It was not invaded, bombed, occupied."

"Do you remember, Jack, what a little bit of bread we had daily during the war?" asked André.

"You bet. Only after Papa came back from the prison camp we were not so badly off at home. Papa went to the country on his bike and smuggled flour. Speaking of Papa, Madame, we had better be going, because if I haven't finished my homework by the time he gets home, brrrrr!"

The boys went to the faucet to get a drink of water. At the Girards', with only Maman to make a living, milk was too expensive to have more than one glass in the morning.

Maman shook hands with Jack and kissed André, saying, "There will be some soup for you when you come back. Just warm it up."

"Madame," said Jack, "if you don't mind, André could eat with us."

André looked at Maman anxiously.

"That's nice of you, Jack, especially since André would be all alone here. But you had better ask your mother first."

"I will, Madame. But I know beforehand it will be yes. Makes no difference, seven or eight people. Just a little more water in the soup!"

They all laughed—even André, who had looked morose ever since Maman's statement that he could not be a racer.

Soon they were at Jack's apartment. It was as old and shabby and spotless as the Girards' place. And, in addition, it was crowded and lively. Miquette was ten, the twins were six, and the baby three.

Miquette said at once, "And the *Tour*? Did you get a look at the papers?"

Round Mrs. Renout, hands on her hips, said affectionately to André, "So, White Rabbit, you've come to help my Jack. That's fine. You will have supper with us, won't you? And you, the others, keep quiet now. Jack and André have work to do."

André and Jack bent over the problem, André explained it over and over again. He never seemed to lose patience. At long last Jack got it. Tentatively he wrote the whole thing on the back of an old envelope. Finally he copied it carefully, in ink, in his notebook. It said this—except, of course, that it was written in French.

When the second racer starts, the first one has already covered 18/2m = 9 miles.

The second racer covers 24 — 18 = 6 more miles per hour.

So it will take him 9/6 = 1 hr. 30 min. to catch up with the first racer.

At that time the second racer will have covered 24m × 1 hr. 30 min. = 36 miles. Therefore he will be 145m — 36m = 109 miles from Le Havre.

And it will be 6 hr. 30 min. + 1 hr. 30 min. = 8 o'clock.

Then they studied their geography assignment, and just as they finished, Mr. Renout came in. He was a powerful-looking man with a ruddy complexion. He wore dark brown corduroy pants, a light tan shirt open at the neck, and a wide blue flannel belt. Most of the ditch-diggers wore that kind of belt—fiery red or cobalt blue—a large strip of flannel to protect the kidneys from the cold and dampness of the soil. As he came in, a broad smile on his face, he handed one end of the cloth to Mrs. Renout; then he spun around while Mrs. Renout unwound the material quickly, until they both bumped into each other, laughing. He kissed her. Then he turned to the children and hugged one after the other, asking, "Have you been wise?"—which is the French way of saying "Have you been good?"

When he came to André, the boy extended his hand, but Mr. Renout boomed, "Don't you kiss me?"

How wonderful it was to be held in Mr. Renout's strong arms! And, later, how great to be sitting at a table with seven people, a man at the head of it. It was so jolly that it made everything taste twice as good: the vegetable soup called *julienne,* the yards of crisp loaves, the salad in a bowl, the Port Salut cheese, and a fistful of cherries. This was supper. The main meal of the day was at noon, when Mr. Renout came back from work for the two-hour lunch period.

Mr. Renout said, "Well, as far as we know tonight, the Swiss are ahead. Of course we will get all the details tomorrow morning in *L'Equipe* or *Le Parisien Libéré.*"

Jack looked at André with questioning eyes, and André understood and said aloud, "I have a picture of Bobet." Everybody wanted to see it, and André got up and took it out of his schoolbag. Miquette read the inscription slowly and repeated, " 'Future bicycle-racer'!"

André blushed, but no one noticed it because the baby was banging her spoon on her high-chair tray, yelling, "Bo! Bo! Bo!"

Mrs. Renout laughed so much that her eyes shut tight and seemed to disappear altogether in her head. "No, no, my little cabbage! *Bo-bet! Bo-bet!* Don't you get so excited; you're not going to marry him."

"Maybe she will marry a cyclist," said André.

"That is most likely," Madame Renout approved. "Who does not ride a bicycle in France, will you tell me? Where is the man who at one time or another has not entered a bicycle contest? Frenchmen are fans of the *Tour* —all of them, practically. Don't you remember, Papa, when you courted me and the only treat you could think of was to let me stand with you for three hours along the

curb under the hot July sun, waiting for the *Tour* racers
to go by?"

Papa laughed. "But, my Big One, you told me you were
interested!"

"Naturally! What else could I say?"

"I don't want to marry just a cyclist," said Miquette. "I
want to marry a real racer."

"Do you really, Miquette?" inquired André anxiously.

"Miquette," said Papa, "you are too young to know
your own mind. It's a tough life, the life of a racer." He
looked at André thoughtfully. " 'Future bicycle-racer.'
Well, maybe you will change your mind later."

"No, sir, I won't."

"I won't either," said Jack.

"All right! All right!" said Papa gaily. His eyes still
resting on André, he added, "Well then, what about
some extra vitamins for these two future bicycle-racers?
What about some milk? And a double glass for André,
because—because he is our guest. Eh, what do you say,
my Big One?" he asked, turning toward Mrs. Renout.

Jack and André sipped the precious liquid slowly,
while the other children watched silently, hands folded
on the table. Suddenly Jack said, "Fernand is getting a
bike for the coming New Year."

"Well, I'll be darned!" said Papa, smacking the table
with his fist.

All at once the twins clapped their hands and chanted,
"He will break his neck, break his neck, break his neck!"

Swiftly Mrs. Renout reached across the table and

tapped them lightly on the head. "Shut up! Such noise! And you should not say such a thing—ever. Even about Fernand."

The twins shed a tear, just to play their part, but they knew very well that nobody was really angry at them. Fernand was very unpopular in the Renout household, since he had once tramped deliberately on a train the twins had made out of small cardboard boxes and were pulling along carefully on La Mouff's sidewalk.

"Well," said Papa forcefully, "if ever Fernand wants to become a professional racer he will have to change his ways a lot. Nowadays a big bicycle road race is not run individually. That was in the old days. Now a race is teamwork. You have to get along with others, you've got to cooperate. Like everything else in our present world, what counts is solidarity."

Jack gave André a friendly kick under the table. Just what he had said this afternoon in class! André kicked back. Solidarity! Didn't the two of them and Michel know about that?"

III. Three and a Thief

André was eating his lunch with Maman. Maman could see he had something on his mind, but she did not press questions on him. André was like her: he did not speak easily. So Maman waited.

It was almost time for André to go back to school when he said, "Maman, when do you think you can buy me the bicycle?"

"Next year, André, as I told you before. For your graduation. When you get your diploma, your *Certificat d'Etudes*. You know I have been saving for three years now. So, if all goes well—work, health, and if you graduate—"

"And if I don't graduate? If I fail?"

"Fail to graduate! You cannot do that, André! You know very well what it would mean: that you would have to quit school. You could not go on studying."

"I don't want to go on studying. I want to go to work, like Jack."

"It's Jack's hard luck that he has to."

"We have no money either. It would be better if I worked."

"We have no money, but you are more gifted than Jack is at studying, and there is a chance that you will get a scholarship. That is fortunate because, as I told you before, you do not have Jack's physique and could not stand a factory job."

That again! André felt as if he had been stabbed. All Fernand's name-calling came back to him. Of course Maman did not know about this. All these years he had never told her what a horrible time he had at school. Maman had just meant to state a fact, but he refused to accept it.

He said defiantly, "I have no need of a scholarship. I want to be a professional racer."

"We won't discuss that now," Maman said firmly. "The truth is that even if you were to be a racer you still could have an education. For several years to come, bicycle-training would not take all your time. You know that it has to be done very gradually."

André asked darkly, his hand on the doorknob, "And if I don't graduate, won't you buy me a bicycle just the same?"

"Certainly not. And you wouldn't want one, either. You would feel ashamed to get one."

Yes, Maman was right, he would feel ashamed, André thought on his way back to school. So he had to graduate. And that meant making a very special effort in grammar. Grammar was his weakest subject. And he would, now that he knew for sure that he would not get his bicycle otherwise. Ever since he could remember, it had been his one wish: to have a bicycle and race in the *Tour*. Let anyone expect him to change his mind! He would not. No indeed! He would show them—Fernand, everybody, including Maman!

He was so absorbed in his thinking that he almost bumped into Michel, who was carrying a pile of notebooks—the grammar ones!—on the heels of Mr. Valeur. Michel winked at André.

Mr. Valeur went into the school building first and said to Michel, "Thank you very much, Mayer. It was nice of you to offer to carry these for me. Just put them on my desk in the classroom."

The bell rang and they all went in.

Mr. Valeur announced, "Boys, here are your corrected grammar notebooks. Some of you who are excellent pupils in everything else don't seem to make a real effort when it comes to grammar. This is very serious. For instance, André Girard. Get up, please."

André got up slowly.

"Girard, I am sorry to say that at the end of the school year your work in grammar is no better than it was at the

beginning. You have not made a bit of progress. Now, my
boy, watch out. Unless you buckle down and really work,
you will flunk the Certificate next year. Do you understand?"

"Yes, sir."

"To speak and write good French," Mr. Valeur went
on, "is very necessary to everybody—even to those bicycle-racers who are uppermost in our minds these days.
Yes indeed! You all look surprised, but I am telling you
the truth. Nowadays a racer has to make speeches; he is
interviewed by newspaper reporters; he talks on the radio; and he probably will be appearing on television soon.
He has to read and answer his fan mail, he is entertained
in high places, he mingles with racers of other countries,
many of whom are well educated. You don't want to
sound like an ignoramus when you rub elbows with ambassadors and cabinet members, do you, Girard?"

André gulped. "No, sir."

"Well then, study your grammar. I said all this, Girard,
since I take it that your ambition is to become a professional racer."

There was a slight sneering noise from Fernand's direction, but it was covered up by the forceful "Yes, sir!"
from André.

"And apparently," said Mr. Valeur, "you are so interested in the *Tour* that you collect items about it. I hear
that you have an autographed picture of Bobet. Is that
correct?"

"Yes, sir."

"Could I see it?"

There! Smart Michel! André took the picture to Mr. Valeur's desk, and while coming back to his seat he looked at Michel knowingly. Michel winked back, a tiny wink. André caught a glimpse of Jack, who was crossing his eyes in such a funny grimace that André almost burst out laughing. It was fortunate that Mr. Valeur was busy looking at Bobet's picture!

As all the boys went out later, at recess time, they were able to get a good look at the picture. Mr. Valeur had it tacked carefully on the wall near the door, with thumb-tacks at the four corners holding it without making any holes in it.

So Jack's idea had worked: André's picture of Bobet was a pinup! Such an honor for André! And all because of clever Michel. In the yard André was surrounded by an admiring crowd; even boys from other grades who had heard about the pinup of the famous racer were there. Fernand, looking like a thundercloud, tried to divert their attention with a bicycle catalogue he had brought.

"Show it to your uncle!" Jack called merrily as he tried to squeeze through the crowd and reach André, who was with Michel at the center of the group. Then Jack felt a hand on his shoulder, and Mr. Valeur said, "Renout, be so good as to take this note to the principal right away." Jack did not want to leave, but of course he had to.

Meanwhile André was trying to answer all the questions about the picture at once. Soon the bell rang, and

André was the last one in line. And then he noticed that everybody was looking in the same direction. He looked too, and he saw that where Bobet's picture had been before recess, there was just the wall—an empty space. The photograph of Bobet was gone.

His heart leaped. He turned to Mr. Valeur. Mr. Valeur looked very stern. He had what the boys called his "bulldog mug." There was an ominous silence as they sat down.

"Boys," said Mr. Valeur, "somebody has played a joke on Girard. One of you has taken down the picture of Bobet and hidden it. Whoever did this must bring it to my desk at once, in which case no one will be punished. I give you one minute to make up your mind."

He took out his watch and set it on the desk. *Tick, tick, tick.* André hid his head in his arms on his desk. His heart was pounding in his ears as if his head were going to burst. The seconds dropped evenly in the silence. No one moved.

"Time is up!" called Mr. Valeur. "Surely one of you has the picture. Come on, boys. This is not only a bad joke, it is stealing."

The class grew tense.

"If the culprit does not give himself up, I shall have to search all of you."

Silence. Silence.

"Very well." Mr. Valeur sighed. "Will you all open the lids of your desks all the way back."

They did, and Mr. Valeur went through each desk carefully. But he did not find a thing. He shook his head.

"All right. Then I shall have to go through your schoolbags. Boys, I hate to do that."

By this time André had tears in his eyes. Mr. Valeur searched one row after another. It was a long, tedious, embarrassing process. Suddenly Mr. Valeur's eyes bulged. He held the picture in his hand. He had found it—in Jack's schoolbag!

Jack's eyes popped out and he shrieked, "I didn't do it! I didn't do it! Honest, sir, I didn't!" and he collapsed on his seat. André looked as if he had been hit on the head.

Mr. Valeur mopped his brow and went back to his desk. He said, "Renout, will you explain the presence of the picture in your schoolbag."

"I can't, sir. I don't know! I didn't put it there!"

"Who did, then? It was your schoolbag, was it not?"

"Yes, sir. But I swear that I didn't put the picture in it."

"But who did, then?"

"I don't know, sir."

"Didn't I send you to the principal with a note during recess time?"

"Yes, sir."

"So you were in the building during recess time?"

"Yes, sir."

"Did you see anyone else?"

Jack sighed. "No, sir, I did not."

Mr. Valeur wore a sad expression as he turned toward Michel. "Mayer, you are the one who mentioned to me, while carrying my notebooks, that Girard had a picture of Bobet. You asked me what I thought about putting it on the wall for all to see. Is that correct?"

"Yes, sir," said Michel with a worried look.

"Was that your own idea, Mayer?"

"Well, sir, I thought—that is—"

"That's enough, Mayer. I can see that it was not your idea. Was it yours, Renout, by any chance?"

"It was, sir, but I did not do it, sir! I did not! André—"

"I am willing to believe you, Renout, but who did it, then? Now, boys, it is up to you to clear Renout. Let the one among you who took the picture stand up and say, 'It is I.'"

No one made a move.

"Boys, you understand what this means. The picture has been found in Renout's bag. He was in the building during recess time. And he is the one who had the idea of having the picture displayed on the wall. Now, he may not be the one who took it, and yet, because of the evidence and because we have no other clue, Renout has to be considered as the culprit. Therefore I have to ask you, Renout, to take your things and move down to the last desk in the room."

"Sir, sir," André begged, raising his hand, "please, sir!"

"Girard, I know perfectly well what you are going to say. You can be sure that this whole thing is just as distasteful to me as it is to you; but it cannot be helped."

And so a day which had started so brightly ended wretchedly.

At long last they were out. Quickly André stepped out on the curb in front of the school and waited for Jack. Jack came out and started to run ahead full speed, without looking to the right or the left.

"Jack! Jack! Wait for me!" yelled André. But Jack kept running. André ran faster; then he cupped his hands and shouted, "Jack! Jack! I—*don't*—believe it!"

And Jack came to a stop so suddenly that André had to slide in order to break his own run. He smiled, but Jack, when he turned around, was not smiling. He looked very angry as he sputtered, "Save your breath. I don't need kind words. I want justice."

And with that he was off again.

André remained rooted to the spot. What had happened? How could Jack have talked to him that way— Jack, his good friend Jack? He leaned against the wall of a house. He felt like crying. Now he wished he had never, never had that picture of Bobet. Utter misery swept over him as he stood alone. A group of boys went past him, but he did not see them. And all at once he heard Fernand's rasping voice.

"My word! It's little André! Just look at him! I thought it was an old lady. What's the matter? Feeling rotten, eh? Your friend Jack is just a yellow dog!"

"He is not a yellow dog!" yelled André.

"Oh yes, he is. A yellow dog! A yellow dog!"

"He is not!" André cried, dropping his schoolbag on the curb and doubling up his fists.

"He is! He is!" snarled Fernand, smiling nastily. "Come on, insignificant insect! Come on! Fight for that thief, that yellow dog!"

Jumping like a wildcat, André landed with such an impact on Fernand that they both lost their balance, fell, and rolled to the curb. Fernand grabbed André's head and pounded it on the cement.

"The teachers, the teachers!" screamed the boys standing around, and everybody started to run. André and Fernand were up in the twinkling of an eye, and running too, as fast as they could, but in different directions.

Around a street corner André stopped. He was out of breath, his hair was tousled, and his clothes were dirty and torn. Jack was nowhere in sight. There were hurried steps around the corner, and André braced himself. It was Michel. What a relief! Michel put his hand on André's shoulder and they started walking together.

Michel said, "Just came in time to hear Fernand's last words and see you sailing through the air and landing square on him. Beautiful! Say, André, are they all like you in that country of yours—Brittany—flaring up so quickly and fist-hitting so well?"

"Wouldn't you have done the same?"

"No. I would have done it the Parisian way: talked and got mad and talked and got mad and so on—not fought at once like that. And that Fernand, he is a steamshovel, and he has no honor. He might have crippled you. Talking is better."

"Talk!" said André bitterly. "I had rather have Jack hit me than talk the way he did."

André told Michel more of what had happened. Michel was thoughtful a while, and then he said, "You can't blame Jack for acting that way. You have the advantage."

"What? I? The advantage?"

"Sure. You got your picture back. You are the one who was wronged. So you are on top, really. You can well afford to be generous, and even that is gravy, so to speak. Just put yourself in Jack's shoes."

"Am I dumb!" cried André. "Of course! You're right, Old One. Never thought of it. To say to Jack that I don't believe it, that just makes *me* feel good. I've got to *prove* that I'm his friend. I've got to get him out of that mess. Michel, how can we do it?"

"Don't know. The way things look, it's kind of hard."

"We've got to fight!" said André passionately.

"Who? You seem to forget we don't know who did it."

André sighed. They walked in silence. Suddenly Michel stopped and said, "I know. We've got to fight, all right, but with our gray matter, see?"

"But how?"

"Well, there are fingerprints, of course. If we could have your picture of Bobet examined we could see whose fingers handled it."

"But Michel, then we would have to have the whole class fingerprinted in order to find out who did it. And besides, by now there are probably too many fingerprints on the picture, including my own and Mr. Valeur's."

Michel nodded. "Right you are, and anyway, maybe the guilty one was smart and used his handkerchief to handle the picture."

They walked on quietly. "Let's think about it overnight," André said as they parted in front of his house. "We've got to find a way."

Maman looked at André's torn clothes, the dirt on his face, and his disheveled hair. She said, "André, when will you understand that this is not Brittany? In Paris boys do not fight at the drop of a hat."

"It was not the drop of a hat. He said something he should not have said!"

"Son, whatever others say about us isn't important enough to make us—"

"And when they say something about a friend?" challenged André.

Maman did not answer.

André laughed shortly. "Well, he did not speak for nothing, anyhow!"

"Who is 'he'?"

"Fernand."

Maman gasped. "Fernand! But you are mad, André, mad! Fernand is twice your—" She stopped abruptly as she saw anger spreading on her son's face, and then she inquired, "What on earth was it about?"

"Jack."

"About Jack?"

"Yes. He called him a yellow dog."

André was silent, and Maman knew better than to ask him for more details. She just said quietly, "I see. As far as name-calling is concerned, it is bad. Always. No matter the name."

Good. Maman understood. André let it go at that. He was cautious; for by saying more he might disclose what he himself had suffered all these years. So he did not mention Bobet's picture, or Jack's behavior in the street. Maybe he would later. Maybe. If he found the clue.

IV. Detectives

Next morning, on his way to school, André caught up with Michel. "Got any bright ideas?"

"Maybe. Look."

Michel pulled a small toy out of his pocket. It was an acrobat on a barrel. The barrel rolled, yet the little wooden figure never fell.

"Oh, Michel, how lovely! But I don't see how it can help us out."

"Well, I'm going to take the chance that the one who stole your picture will also want this."

"Why would he?"

"Because I bet I'm going to be awfully popular with this little toy—you watch! So maybe he will want it."

"Perhaps. But then how do we know that the skunk

65

won't slip it in somebody else's bag, perhaps even Jack's? Then we would be in a pretty fix!"

"Sure. But that's where you and I come in, my friend. We are going to be detectives."

Michel had foreseen right. As soon as he showed his little acrobat in the schoolyard there was a crowd of boys around, and by the time the bell rang Michel had become the center of attraction.

At recess time he opened his desk wide enough for everyone back of him to see that he was leaving the toy right there. Everybody went out into the yard.

"What next?" whispered André.

"Well, I tell you, we've got to watch both entrances to the building. You go back and hide under the steps. I'll stay in front and hide behind a tree. The one who sees someone going into the building comes to warn the other. Then, if we are lucky and old Valeur's back is turned, we sneak inside after the robber. By that time he will have reached the classroom and we can catch him red-handed."

"Okay," said André.

"Now just don't look as if we were planning something. Let's lose ourselves in the crowd and go to our posts without making any fuss."

They did; and finally André hid under the back steps and Michel took up his watch behind a tree in front of the school.

Presently André heard soft, quick footsteps going up the stairs. Someone was climbing lightly, and he was in a hurry. He was already opening the door. Quickly but cautiously André shot a glance in his direction. He caught sight of a boy just closing the door softly. It was Jack!

André suppressed a shriek. No, no! It couldn't be! But it was. It was Jack—no one else. Jack! André felt cold all over; he was rooted to the spot. Now he should run and warn Michel. But he couldn't move. Before he had had time to recover, he saw Michel running toward him. Michel grabbed his hand and said, "Quick, quick! Old V. is not looking!" And they raced up the steps. André felt sick to his stomach. So Michel had seen Jack too! And now— His head was in a whirl. Blindly he kept up with Michel as they ran through the hall on tiptoe. And here they were at the classroom door. Michel put a finger on his lips, and very quietly turned the knob, and—bang! —the door burst open.

And there was—Fernand, just taking the toy acrobat out of Michel's desk. A wild yell rang through the class-room, and a form sprang from behind Mr. Valeur's desk. Jack! So Michel had seen Fernand entering the building, and André had seen Jack.

Just then the bell rang and Mr. Valeur walked in with the principal.

Later, when everything had been explained and the principal had left, after saying, "Fausset, you report to my office within fifteen minutes," Mr. Valeur said to Fernand, "Fausset, since you insist that you only wished to have a close look at Mayer's acrobat, we shall let it go at that. We have plenty to talk about if we confine ourselves to Girard's picture episode. It was silly to take it off the wall. But had you just done that—even hidden it for a while to play a trick on Girard—it would not have been serious. But you arranged it so that the blame would fall on somebody else, and, worse, you let that person stand accused.

"I want you to think about that for a few minutes. You are smart, very smart, Fausset. Probably the only thing you are sorry about just now is that you let yourself be caught. And you are promising yourself not to make the same mistake twice. Maybe you won't. Maybe you will keep cool, and have your wits about you, and squirm out of it."

The class was tense, especially Fernand's admirers, who had often heard him use exactly that kind of language.

"Now the point is this," Mr. Valeur went on firmly, but not without kindness, "how long will you go scot-free? Maybe for quite a time. But someday it will catch up with you, and just when you expect it the least. In a bicycle race, for instance."

The class was so quiet that you could have heard a pin drop. Mr. Valeur went on, "A few days ago you said you wanted to be a bicycle-racer—in order to make money, I believe. Well, how would you like, for instance, to find yourself suddenly disqualified in the *Tour de France* because of cheating? That's what might happen to you if you go on acting the way you have. You'd better change your ways, my boy, while there is still time. Mark my words: cheating, bullying, and outwitting people with smooth, sly smartness or ruthless means will not get you very far as a racer. Neither will money, in spite of what you may think. The motto for the racers of the *Tour de France* is solidarity. The sooner you realize it, the better for you. And now go and report to the principal."

When Fernand came back he handed a piece of paper to Mr. Valeur on which the principal had written that Fernand was suspended for the rest of the school year. Though this was a bad mark, Fernand was not upset, as there were only a few days left. He was not bothered by his failure either. He had failed in his attempt to get even with Jack and to break up Jack's friendship with André. But there would be plenty of other opportunities, and, no doubt, far better ones. So with cool unconcern he gathered his belongings, and, without so much as a word or a nod, left the classroom. Mr. Valeur made no further comment when he was gone, but everybody seemed to breathe more easily.

André could hardly wait until school was over. He could not see Jack's face, because Jack was sitting in the front row again, and there had been no time to talk when Fernand was caught.

At long last school was out, and there on the curb was Jack, waiting. He was beaming, but he looked a little sheepish. André rushed to him, and they shook hands vigorously.

"I'll never, never forget it!" Jack kept repeating. "Never, do you hear me? Not as long as I live!"

"It was Michel's plan," said André.

"Fiddlesticks!" said Michel, who had joined them. "It was your idea to fight to the hilt. I only supplied a little scheme."

"André, you're a brick! And to think that I gave you the brushoff yesterday."

"And you should have seen him landing on Fernand, right after!"

"Yes, I heard about it. André, you—"

"Oh, forget it, both of you. You would have done the same. Solidarity, you know—like in the *Tour,* as old V. said."

"But what I don't understand," said Michel, "is how you, Jack, happened to be in the classroom too."

"Well, I figured out that the thief of the picture might want that toy too, so it would be a good way to catch him and clear myself at the same time."

"Correct. Only you forgot that had you been alone with him—that is, with Fernand—he might have been the one to accuse you."

"Right! Without you two witnesses I would have been sunk again! But then— André, you must have seen *me* going up the steps!"

André nodded.

"Oh la la la la!" cried Jack, rolling his eyes and shaking his left hand. He put his arm affectionately around André's thin shoulders. Then as the three of them proceeded down the street, arm in arm, he added, laughing, "You and big Fernand! Must have been some sight! Now don't hit the sidewalk again with that Breton head of yours. You might break the curb next time."

"A head like that," said Michel thoughtfully, "would be mighty helpful in the *Tour*."

The *Tour!* The beloved *Tour,* which had nearly caused a break in their friendship.

That year Bobet covered eighteen stretches before he scored in a spectacular flight in the Izoard pass of the Alps.

In November, on André's namesake day, Saint André, Maman gave him a fancy frame for Bobet's picture. André hung it above his bed.

V. Graduation Ahead

There were two gay weeks for André that summer, when Maman had her paid vacation. They went back to Maman's village on the Brittany coast, and the hotel owner asked very little for their room and board because he knew Maman and he felt sorry for her, being so young and a widow and having to work so hard in the post office.

The beach was beautiful, and when Maman and André were tired of the seashore they could take long walks through the countryside, which was covered with heather, Druid ruins, old chapels, wishing wells, and roadside shrines. On the roads they met big buses full of tourists. Maman and André could not afford the fare for the sight-seeing buses.

If only we had bicycles, like so many people! Well, next year I shall, thought André, and his heart jumped.

But even without bicycles the two-week vacation went too fast, and André found himself back in Paris for the rest of the summer. It was hot, and he was lonesome. Jack had been sent to a camp for large families. Michel was in the mountains—at Grandpa Isaac's, he had said; though Mr. Isaac was no blood relation of his, but the father of Michel's adopted mother, Mrs. Morel. André felt cooped up in the apartment. He wished he could get away from the heat, from the city. If only he had a bicycle!

That was it. A bicycle was not just the first, indispensable requirement for his becoming a racer. All by itself, a bicycle spelled independence, freedom, adventure, the joy of the open road, the possession of the outer world simply through one's own muscular effort. A train, a car, takes you somewhere. But on a bicycle you take yourself. André could become familiar with the whole countryside, could learn every inch of the way, by his own physical exertion. And in addition, later on, he could pick up his father's challenge and race in the *Tour*. And—

Well, next year. Next year he would be free to move about, and he would be on his way toward his goal. "If nothing goes wrong," Maman said. What could possibly go wrong? Maman could get sick. But Maman enjoyed good health. André could not remember her missing one day's work, ever. And since Maman worked in the post office, there was little chance of her being out of work—unlike Mr. Renout and Mr. Morel, who had manual jobs on various construction projects, and were sometimes un-employed. No, he couldn't think of anything that might prevent him from getting his bike, except if, through his own fault, he failed to graduate. But he was going to work like a Trojan at grammar, and graduate!

At long last October, and the reopening of school, came once again. André was overjoyed, not only because he had been lonesome, but because each day would bring him nearer his dream. He could see at the end of the school-year trail his bicycle, standing on a pinnacle, sur-rounded by a halo. Paradise on wheels!

"Hello, Jack!" André called joyfully in the street. "What a tan you have!"

"Oh, André, I wish you had been there! Believe it or not, I rode a bike!"

"You did!"

"Yes, the director of the camp had one. He was an aw-fully nice young chap, very tall. So he held the bike for me first, because my feet couldn't reach the pedals. Then he gave me a push, and I stayed right on. I actually rode quite a little way several times."

André's eyes shone. His friend Jack had ridden. It made him feel closer to his own bike.

Someone behind them whistled the popular march *Sambre et Meuse*. They turned around. Michel! They shook hands happily.

"Ah," said Michel, "you both should have been at my Grandpa Isaac's! A regular pal. I helped him to make *Tomme* cheese and went with him in his delivery truck to sell it. And we always had wonderful talks while driving, mostly about the *Tour*. Believe it or not, what he doesn't know about the *Tour* isn't worth mentioning. He gets all excited when he speaks about it, and he shouts, '*Sambre et Meuse! Sambre et Meuse!*' "

They laughed. They knew about *Sambre et Meuse,* of course—who does not in France? The Sambre and the Meuse are two rivers on the French eastern border, where over and over again throughout the centuries the French had fought and defeated the invaders. After a spectacular victory in 1794 a song praising the particular regiment which had fought then had sprung up in France, and the title soon became synonymous with brave, astonishing deeds.

Sambre et Meuse fitted the *Tour* perfectly. The boys hummed the tune gaily as they went on talking about the two beloved subjects: bicycles and the *Tour*.

"Look at Fernand over there!" cried André. "He's got a leather schoolbag."

"And look at the crowd of suckers around him! They have forgotten all about last year's performance. Money, money!" chanted Jack, rolling his eyes.

"Too bad we can't have old Valeur again this year," Michel remarked.

"Wonder what kind of chap the seventh-grade teacher is?"

Jack held his nose conspicuously as they went in, and Michel and André nodded understandingly.

The new teacher meant business. He pointed out to the

boys that so far in his long career he had never registered a failure at the national graduation examination, and he was not going to start now. So they might just as well make up their minds to work hard.

For most boys the following year became a nightmare from which there was no possible escape. In addition, the winter was exceptionally severe. The lake in the Bois de Boulogne froze. André, Jack, and Michel went to see it. They longed to skate.

Jack said, "I have an idea. What about asking our parents to pool their money and buy *one* pair of skates for the three of us? We could take turns."

"You forget one little item," said Michel mildly. "We don't wear the same size shoes."

"Anyway," said André, "I couldn't possibly ask my mother for a penny. She's saving it all for my bike."

"If you get your C.E.," Michel put in.

"Sure. Michel," André asked suddenly, "will *you* get a bike? You never told us."

Michel said lightly, "Maybe yes, maybe no." And he chuckled as if he were tickled. André and Jack looked puzzled. Sometimes Michel was so mysterious that you couldn't make him out.

Jack asked, "But you do want to be a racer, don't you?"

"There is nothing I would like better," said Michel warmly.

On their way home they took the Avenue de la Grande

Armée, because it is full of bicycle stores. Abruptly they came to a stop in front of a window. There in the center, all by itself, stood the object of their dreams: a racing bicycle. They held their breath. Each one could picture himself on it, pedaling furiously on the last stretch of the *Tour* and victoriously entering the Paris stadium, the Parc des Princes; then slowly making his tour around the track after having donned the golden pullover, while forty thousand spectators went wild with enthusiasm.

After a while André sighed and whispered, "Isn't she elegant?"

"Smart!" approved Jack. "I bet she doesn't weigh more than twenty pounds."

"See the cute feeding bottle," said Michel, pointing with his finger. "Right in front, so you can drink as you go."

"And look how well you can see the working of the gear shift," André added.

Michel asked, "How do you like that color—transparent blue?"

"Lovely," said Jack, "especially with yellow rims."

"And yellow handlebars," André put in.

"And everything shining chromium-plated. A real honey!" Michel sighed in admiration.

"I wonder what kind of model Fernand is going to get for the New Year," mused Jack.

They were soon to know. As they were on their way to school the day after New Year's Fernand brushed past them so close to the curb that André was nearly knocked down. Immediately an admiring circle formed around Fernand, and there were pleading voices from many boys. "Fernand, give me a ride! Just one! One little one! Please!" But Fernand would not give anybody a ride; he would not even seat small boys on the saddle.

It was a beautiful sports bike, just the right size for Fernand—that is, for the time being. Michel, looking at all the disappointed faces around, said to Fernand pointedly, "That bike is not going to last you more than a year —maybe not even that long. You'll outgrow it in no time."

"You are so bright, bookworm," snapped Fernand. "You must be running a fever! Of course I'll outgrow it. What's the difference? My uncle will give me another one, that's all."

All the boys groaned. What? Not only a bike before

graduation, but maybe another one within a few months! Michel said sweetly and distinctly, "I prefer waiting until I can ride a real racing bike." And, hands in his pockets, he withdrew, whistling *Sambre et Meuse*.

Jack picked up the cue immediately. "I prefer waiting until I can buy my own." And, puffing out his cheeks and wrinkling his nose, he made a face at Fernand as he pulled out of the crowd.

Then André chanted, "When *I* get my bike, watch me leave that old tub behind!"

Fernand yelled, "Oh, you will, will you? Little runt! Look at him! That's all they can produce in Brittany, and he has the nerve—"

André, who had already followed Jack and Michel, whirled back and, red with anger, shouted, "Shut your big mouth! The *Tour* has more champs from Brittany than from any other province!"

"Come on," said Michel. "Leave him alone. What do you care?"

It was one thing to put up a front for Fernand's benefit, but when the three friends were walking together again they did not feel so cocky.

"He can start training gradually right away," said Michel.

"He will be ahead of us for years to come," said André.

"And all because his uncle has money. Now is that fair?" said Jack.

"Maybe," André remarked hopefully, "the weather will turn so wet he won't be able to go out for weeks."

Indeed, by the end of January it was slushy, rainy, and windy, at least on the days that were not school days. The three friends could not help thinking that this was a real piece of luck! But one morning late in March, André woke up with the feeling that something disagreeable was about to happen. What could it be? It was Thursday, a free day. He got up and opened the shutters. And then he knew. The air was crisp, the sun shone, and the pavement was dry. What a day for cycling! He stood there in his nightshirt, wishing it would rain cats and dogs!

Suddenly he noticed someone coming down La Mouff', riding a bicycle, with a lunchbag over his shoulder. Fernand! André moved away from the window in a hurry; he didn't want Fernand to see him.

His heart was heavy as he sat down to breakfast. Maman had already left for work. Slowly he dipped his chunk of bread in the milk he had warmed up. But he was not in the apartment any more. He was on the road, on Fernand's bicycle. He was not eating bread; he was devouring miles. He was on his own, and training for the *Tour*.

He came to as he tried to empty the already empty bowl. He was home. It was Thursday, and he had been given an extra assignment, additional grammar homework. Grammar. Grammar. The C.E. His bicycle. Graduation—in a little over three months. He tightened his lips and spread his books on the table. Then he picked up his grammar and read: "Past participles used with the auxiliary verb 'to have' agree with the direct object if the direct object precedes the verb."

How many times for the last three years had he wrestled with that rule? Why was it so difficult for him to apply it? What was wrong with his mind? He remembered bitterly the sarcastic remark the teacher had made the day before, when he had given André the extra assignment—"Girard, get that participle rule through your thick head!" And behind André there had been a sneering whisper from Fernand. "Thick Breton head!"

He slammed his fist on the table. Breton head! All right, he would show them. A bulldozer through obstacles!

VI. Bad News

One evening in April, André was working at the round table, doing his homework. It was just the same as any other evening in early spring, balmy and soft. The window was open, and while wrestling with grammar André could not help thinking that after just about three more months of hard work he would be able to enjoy the lovely weather to the full, riding on his bicycle.

Then Maman came in and said quietly, "We are on strike."

André looked up at her in utter amazement. He was not even sure he had heard right. Maman on strike—as Mr. Renout and Mr. Morel and so many parents of other school children had been in the past? Maman on strike? At the post office? All of a sudden André felt unsafe, fearful, and resentful. He did not want the world around him upset. He was in a real panic.

Maman realized this and sat down by him, saying, "Yes, I know, it is hard. But listen, André, you must understand. There was no other way out. The cost of living is rising all the time. We asked for a raise long ago, and they wouldn't give it to us. So the union, the CFTC, voted to strike at long last; and the other unions followed suit, so all the post-office employees have stopped working."

"How long will it last?" asked André darkly.

"I don't know. Probably until we get better wages."

Suddenly a smile broke through on André's worried face as he asked, "And meanwhile you will stay at home?"

"Of course."

"So you will be home when I come back from school? Every day? Oh, boy! Oh, boy!"

"Yes, son, I'll be home, and that will be nice. But it would be far better if I were not home, if I were working at decent wages. It will go hard with us if the strike lasts."

André went back to school the next day in a turmoil. He felt perturbed but somehow important. Jack rushed up to him, shook hands warmly, and said, "It's tough. But life is like that."

Michel remarked thoughtfully, "It shouldn't be this way—people having to strike to make a living wage."

Many boys who had hardly ever spoken to André before came up and shook hands with him. Because of the strike, he was discovering new friends.

The first week was not bad at all. As a matter of fact, André loved it. It was such a treat to have Maman home. Of course, she had to attend meetings of the union. But she was home when he left for school, and during the lessons he kept remembering that she would be there when he got back. This thought was like a warm glow spreading all through his body; it seemed to make the whole day bright and peaceful.

During the second week Maman began to take longer to do the shopping for the meals. Once she looked quite concerned as she remarked, "We have to save as much as we possibly can. Nobody knows how long the strike will last."

By the third week they had meat only once, on Sunday.

By the fourth week they could not afford even that. Every day they ate the same thing: boiled potatoes at noon and lentil soup at night. André yearned for some green vegetables. And he kept thinking, If only I had a bike. I could go to the country around Paris and gather wild dandelions and watercress. But he had no bike—not yet. And all of a sudden fear gripped his heart. Was the strike slowly eating up Maman's savings?

He did not dare ask.

At first the Renouts and the Morels had invited him to dinner quite often. But as the strike went on, it began to be felt elsewhere. Gradually all the business of the nation slowed down and practically came to a standstill. Soon all the working people were up against it, and they had to dig into their meager savings or go into debt.

At school no one except Fernand held it against André, whose mother's union had started the strike. Fernand was mad and bitter because the closing of the post office had prevented him from getting a box of chocolates from his uncle. But although all the boys suffered from the strike more or less, there was no talk about calling it off.

Michel said to André, "It's just the same as in bicycle-racing: you have to hold on until you reach the goal."

And Jack said tersely, "Solidarity."

André nodded. "Just like in the *Tour*."

The *Tour*. His bicycle. He could not tear his mind from it. Suppose the savings were gone? Then he would go to work. He would have to. That way he could earn money and buy a bicycle, like Jack, and start training. Maman would have to let him.

That night, as he refused a second helping of lentil soup, he said, trying to sound offhand, "Maman, times are too hard. I'll quit school next July and go to work."

Maman flared up at once. "You will do no such thing! If you get your C.E. with honorable mention you can probably be recommended for further schooling."

"I don't care. I'd rather work—like Jack."

Maman said sharply, "I told you a hundred times that's Jack's hard luck. Besides, he is a year older than you are, and as I've said before, you could not do it anyhow. You don't have the physique."

"I could too!" he flung back angrily.

"Stop talking nonsense, André. All this is only a pretext. You just don't want to apply your mind to the one subject that might make you fail to graduate. I have watched you since I've been home, and I know now that you don't work half as hard as you should at grammar. As a matter of fact, lately you have been doing nothing but daydreaming—just as if there was not enough trouble as it is."

André turned his head away and spread his books in front of him. A lump was in his throat. Daydreaming? He felt so tired lately, all the time. And, in addition, for several weeks now he had suffered a great deal because his shoes were getting too short and his toes were all cramped inside them. It was so painful. And then, suppose he were crippled? Toes are so important in bicycle-racing. During the day, whenever he happened to be home alone, he hurried to bathe his feet in cold water.

He would not tell Maman anything. What was the use? Maman's burden was heavy enough without it. But why was she so harsh?

He looked at her sideways. She had picked up his vest and was carefully piecing together longer cuffs on his sleeves. Yes, he had shot up like a slender weed. Why didn't she think of his shoes? But if she had it would not help. Just one more worry. Probably the bottom of the savings had been reached. From under his long eyelashes André peered at her. She had large dark circles under her eyes, and for the first time he noticed that her old sweater, which used to fit her so well, was all loose around her shoulders. He felt a pinch at his heart. Maman must have lost a lot of weight!

He buried himself in his grammar. Suddenly Maman stopped sewing, and opening her eyes wide, as if she were making a fearful discovery, she asked anxiously, "André, what about your shoes?"

He seemed wholly absorbed in his work as he said evenly, "My shoes?"

"Yes, your shoes. This vest has become so short—you have grown so much recently—your shoes must—"

He never lifted his head from his book, and his voice did not waver. "My shoes are all right."

Maman bent forward eagerly. "Your feet don't hurt, I hope?"

He shook his head with a frown, as if Maman were interfering with his work.

"It's strange, André. You should tell me the truth. Are you sure they're all right?"

He nodded emphatically, without looking up.

"Ah," said Maman, and there was almost a trace of gaiety in her voice, "probably you'll be like me: small feet. What a relief! With no end of the strike in sight, where in the world would we find money for shoes just now?"

André did not budge. He seemed utterly lost in his studying. Maman resumed her alteration job. The clock ticked in the silence. How good it would be to slip his poor toes between the cool sheets tonight!

And still the strike went on—and so did school. The teacher kept driving the boys as if the one and only important event in the world were the approaching graduation examination. Once only did he refer to the strike. Then he said dryly, "Let no one among you delude himself. Whatever happens in this country, whether there is war, invasion, occupation, flood, fire, strike, or revolution, nothing has ever changed the requirements for graduation. The examiners never swerve from their standards, and that goes for this year too. So work!"

The strike ended at last, one month before the exam. The raise in salary was not as high as had been asked, yet it was an improvement. Maman, wan as she was, smiled and said to André, "Nothing worth while comes easily in life."

He nodded. Didn't he know it? Nothing—not grammar, not a bike, not even shoes! Warm weather had come, and his feet ached more and more; his concern about being permanently crippled gnawed at his mind.

He did not dare show his joy when at the end of the first week of work Maman said, "It's so hot. What about going to the market to buy you a pair of rope sandals?"

As they neared the market André suggested, "Maman, why don't you go on with your shopping while I look for some sandals?"

"All right. Here is the money. When you are through, meet me at the cheese stand."

Quickly he lost himself in the crowd. He found a rope-sandal display. "What size?" the merchant asked.

"I don't know."

"Show me your foot."

"That doesn't matter," said André firmly. "Please, may I try this navy pair?"

He took off one of his shoes and, leaning against the pole of the stand, he slipped the sandal on. How wonderful it felt! He took off his other shoe and put on the other sandal. They fitted perfectly.

"I'll take them," he said, beaming. "Never mind wrapping them up. I'm going to wear them right away."

The merchant demurred. "All right, but give me your shoes then. I'll find a piece of newspaper to wrap them in."

André handed the man his shoes. "What!" exclaimed the merchant. "But my boy, you were wearing shoes a whole size smaller than the sandals you bought."

André smiled, paid, and hurried away. He felt light as a feather. His poor suffering toes now had all the room they needed. Now he could walk miles. He was not crippled! He was not crippled! And wouldn't the sandals be great for cycling. Cycling! When?

He reached the cheese stand, where Maman was waiting for him. She eyed his shoes critically. "Very nice. But why so big?"

"Oh, I like my sandals large."

"But André, this is not such a good idea. They will become too loose, and you might trip."

Before he knew it, she had bent over, and her finger was on his big toe. She got up abruptly and looked at him, her eyes full of questions. He quietly sustained her stare.

Impetuously she drew him to her, moaning softly, "Oh, my dear, my dear! You are a Breton, all right." Then she released him, turning her face away.

Arm in arm they walked home slowly.

And all the while he had but one thought: I am not crippled! I am not crippled! I will be able to race!

VII. The Great Hope

He knew it. He should not hope. The strike had shattered all possibilities. And yet he could not help it—as the date of the examination neared, his expectations grew. Sometimes he thought, I'll ask Maman pointblank, "Do you have any savings left for the bike?"—no, I'll say it the other way around. I'll say, "Of course, now my bicycle is out of the question." But he never asked. He wanted to go on hoping.

He did not speak to anyone about it, not even to Jack or Michel. It was as if the words could not pass his lips. In his darkest moments, when he faced squarely the fact that he could not possibly expect a bicycle for graduation any more, revolt surged within him so strongly that he clenched his fists and said to himself, I don't care! I will go to work then, in spite of anything Maman says! And maybe she will let me, anyhow.

That was completely ruled out after the teacher called him to his desk one day and said, "Girard, will you tell your mother that the principal would like to talk to her?"

At first Maman had been quite upset. "Did you do anything wrong, André? Why does he want to see me?"

But when she came back from school, she was all aglow. "Oh, André, this is wonderful! The principal says that you are now one of the top pupils and he is going to recommend you for admission to technical school. He said you no longer have any difficulties with grammar. He thinks you will graduate, all right—barring a mishap, of course. He wanted to make sure that I had no objection to your going on with your studies. Can you imagine my objecting? As I told him, it has been my fondest dream. And he said he was glad, because he was afraid I might want you to work, because of my being a widow; and he did not think you should anyway, because you—" She stopped abruptly.

"Because of what?" André asked sharply.

"Because you have enough of a mind to deserve more study," said Maman quickly.

André knew that was not what the principal had said. What the principal had undoubtedly told Maman was, "Because he is not strong enough for physical work." That was it. Well, he would show them someday what Girard's son could do.

The examination was to take place on June twenty-ninth, and the *Tour* that year was scheduled to start on the first of July. Already everyone discussed the prospects and the chances. As time went on, the boys found it hard to keep their minds on their books. These were harrowing weeks. André, Jack, and Michel would get together after supper at one of their homes and quiz one another until late at night. Nobody said anything to them. Fathers and mothers had gone through the same ordeal years before, and they knew that in a world of bitter competition a fair start in life for their children depended primarily on their getting this first diploma.

The days before the exam grew shorter and shorter. All the mothers became very busy, washing, cleaning, and pressing suits. The fathers cut the boys' hair, and the boys tried daily to smooth rebellious strands.

At last it was D-Day. They had to get up very early. The examination started at seven-thirty. It was held in a large municipal building that could accommodate several hundred pupils. In the main hall there were rows and rows of planks resting on sawhorses, to be used as writing tables. Boys were seated five feet apart, and no pupils from the same school sat next to each other. For every examination, each boy was given a large sheet of paper. In the corner he wrote his name. That corner of the sheet had glue on the edge, and when it was folded the other side of it was black. So once it was glued, nobody could see the name, so nobody knew whose composition it was.

All papers were corrected and rated before the names were disclosed. That way it was impossible for any examiner to play favorites.

In a dead silence, the seal of the envelope containing the first test was broken by one of the examiners. The envelope had come directly from the government, so nobody knew what was in it. It was marked on the outside: TEXT FOR DICTATION.

This text was slowly dictated to the boys. It was a test of twelve lines, or about one hundred and fifty words. Ten mistakes, whether of misspelled words, grammatical errors, or incorrect punctuation, were sufficient to make one fail. But a boy would not know he had failed this exam until he had taken all the written tests.

The dictation was followed by three questions, including one on the agreement of the past participle with the object. Just what André had had such a time learning!

The next test was in arithmetic—two problems. Every step in every problem had to be proved by a method known as the "Check by 9."

The next test included a question on history, one on geography, and two on applied science.

By the time they had finished, it was twelve o'clock, and they all hurried out for the two-hour lunch period, as some of them had quite a way to go.

In the afternoon the first test was in composition, which included penmanship. They had a choice between two subjects to write about: they could describe spring; or they could comment on the saying "One is often in need of a person smaller than oneself." The boys were expected to write about four pages on whichever subject they chose. They were given inexpensive yellow paper for the first draft. Then each pupil copied his composition neatly on the large white sheet with the black corner. Of course, the main test was of one's ability to have ideas and to express them well with a clear plan and adequate wording. But grammar counted too. No matter how good a composition was, if there were too many grammatical mistakes the writer would flunk. Penmanship was graded too, and neatness was also taken into consideration.

Every fifteen minutes one of the ushers got up and announced in a deep, fateful voice, "One hour and a half left. . . . One hour and a quarter left. . . ." His voice fell in the silence like a dreaded toll. Some boys wrote fast. Others seemed to struggle. Some looked desperate. It was very hot in the hall, and of course no one would have dared to take off his vest. A boy who did this would be sent away at once for displaying a lack of proper respect for the examiners and the examination itself.

After composition came drawing. A copy of a large, beautiful Greek vase was carried in and set in front of the boys, who had to draw it on special paper.

They were out at four-thirty. Results would not be announced before the next morning at eleven o'clock. André, Jack, and Michel compared notes. André and Jack had chosen to write about spring. Michel had taken the second subject. Jack was very pleased about one of the problems in the arithmetic test. He said, "I saw right away that it was like the problem of the cyclists which you explained to me so well, André, last year."

By ten-thirty the next morning there was a great crowd waiting for the results in the street in front of the hall; and the excitement mounted as time grew shorter. Suddenly there was a dead silence. One fold of the double door had opened, and a man came out with a list, which he proceeded to tack on the closed side of the double door. A mad rush followed, everyone making for that door. Boys pushed and pulled, shouting and yelling to those who had got close to the list, "Look for my name! Did you see my name?" In the confusion André, Jack, and Michel got separated. When they found one another again the three said all together at once, "You passed!" They shook hands happily but briefly, because they did not want to make it harder for those around who had failed. Many boys were sobbing openly and could not bring themselves to leave the place.

The door opened again, and the usher said, "All those who have passed the written part of the exam are expected back here at two o'clock for the oral exam."

The boys dispersed and hurried home for lunch. Fernand whizzed by on his bicycle. Jack said, "He passed too." André nodded, his mind wholly on the bicycle.

They were back at two, a much smaller crowd than in the morning. The hall had been cleared of writing tables. There were just a few tables set around in a large circle; these were labeled: READING, MENTAL ARITHMETIC, REC-ITATION OR SINGING.

Behind each table sat two examiners. On each table there was a shoebox with folded pieces of paper inside. They were the questions to draw. The boys stood in line, waiting their turn. It was just luck. Sometimes you drew an easy question and sometimes a difficult one.

For oral reading there was a text to be read, a text you had never seen before. You had to do it fluently and with the proper pauses and inflection. Then you were asked to close the book and tell in your own words what the passage was all about. Finally the examiner asked you how the passage was composed, how it was planned and developed. If it referred to history he would ask you about that period of history. If it was about general ideas he would ask your opinion of such things as tolerance, cooperation, respect for one's word, honor, understanding of others, and so forth.

There were five mathematical problems to be solved mentally. Then you had to explain how you did it.

You could choose between recitation or singing. Then the examiner made his own choice among the five titles you picked. Jack's examiner was unusually pleasant. He looked at the list of poems that Jack handed him and said, "What would *you* like to recite?"

" 'The Hare and the Tortoise,' sir," Jack answered promptly.

All at once the examiner looked furious and bellowed, "I am sick and tired of that 'Hare and Tortoise'! What is the matter with you? Why do you all want to recite that today? Answer me! Why?"

Jack said meekly, "Well, sir, it's because of the *Tour*."

"The tour of what?" shouted the examiner. "Are you being fresh now?"

"The *Tour de France,* sir," Jack said quietly. He had never been so scared in his life. Suppose the examiner flunked him!

But the examiner looked mellow as he said, "Ah, I see. I have been teaching abroad for so long I had forgotten. Of course, my boy, let us have 'The Hare and the Tortoise.' "

Jack cleared his throat.

> "If you don't start on time, you might as well not try:
> As proved by the tortoise when a boaster finished last.
> 'Wager who'll be the winner?' . . ."

André was not as lucky as Jack. His examiner picked the most difficult poem: "Temps Futurs" by Victor Hugo. André swallowed hard, but he went ahead bravely.

> "Behold: The sublime vision!
> The Peoples have arisen from the abyss.
>
> From henceforth the eye that gazes upward
> Distinctly sees this beautiful Dream
> Which one day shall become Reality;
> For God shall destroy every chain,
> The Past shall be called Hatred
> And the Future called Love.
>
> In the depths of the skies a twinkling point of light is seen.
> Look: it grows, it shines,

It draws near, enormous, vermilion.
O Universal Republic,
Thou art still a spark but
Tomorrow Thou shalt be the Sun."

"Very good, very good indeed," the examiner said. "Somebody who recites that poem so well ought to go on studying. Are you?"

"Yes, sir," answered André without enthusiasm.

"What's the matter? You don't seem pleased. Why is that? What do you want to do in life eventually?"

André reddened. "I want to be a bicycle-racer, sir."

"A bicycle-racer!"

"Yes, sir. In the *Tour*."

"But my boy, you are not cut out for that at all! One needs a physique"—the examiner scanned the room and pointed to a boy a few tables away—"a physique like that boy over there, for instance." André looked in the direction in which the examiner's finger was pointing. It was Fernand!

André frowned, bent his head, and said, "I know what you mean, sir. But I want to be a racer."

The examiner shrugged his shoulders. "Don't take it so hard. I just meant that you have what it takes to go on for a better education. Next candidate."

The examiner shaded his right hand with his left as he wrote down André's mark, but André saw the movement of his fingers, and they spelled out the figure ten. The highest possible mark! André smiled. Of course he would make it! Of course he would be a racer!

At that moment the whole room was startled by the stirring strains of a song. *Sambre et Meuse!*

> "The Sambre et Meuse Regiment
> Always answers liberty's call,
> Against us they were hundreds of thousands,
> And in command were kings."

Michel! He had chosen to sing instead of reciting.

"Hum, hum," said the examiner, clearing his throat, as if he had been doing the singing himself. "Good rhythm and a lot of feeling. Now what do you know about the Sambre et Meuse Regiment? Why that name?"

"The Sambre and the Meuse are two rivers on the French eastern border. In 1794 the poor revolutionary French army fought and defeated there the well-trained, well-equipped armies of all Europe."

"Right. Can you think of another time when the French defeated the invader along the line of the Sambre and Meuse rivers?"

"Yes, sir, in the First World War. And in the Second World War the Americans fought victoriously along the Meuse in the Battle of the Bulge."

"Good. Now tell me, when you hear that phrase *Sambre et Meuse,* what does it mean to you?"

Michel said with conviction, "Courage in the face of tremendous odds and obstacles."

"Excellent." The examiner smiled. "I am going to give you a good mark. However, my advice is: lay off singing for a while, my boy. Your voice is changing."

By four o'clock it was all over. The boys were told to leave the hall. Results would be posted at six o'clock.

They walked outside, and there on the sidewalk was a dignified old gentleman with a curly white beard.

"Grandpa Isaac!" shouted Michel. What a surprise!

"Sambre et Meuse!" shouted the elderly gentleman, clasping Michel in his arms. "You don't think I would miss such an event, do you? Came all the way in my delivery truck."

He shook hands with André and Jack. "So happy to meet you. I've heard a lot about you from Michel, of course. And, by the way, was it you, Michel, singing my favorite song, *Sambre et Meuse?* I heard it clearly!"

Michel nodded happily.

"Good, good! That pleases me no end," said Grandpa Isaac genially. "That's a song to stir the spirit of every young French boy—like me, for instance, no?"

The boys laughed.

"Tsk, tsk, tsk," said Grandpa Isaac. "I am young enough to know exactly the way you feel now. And I'll bet you're famished! What do you say we repair to a pastry shop? We have plenty of time before the final results."

The boys were delighted. As they entered the shop Grandpa Isaac said, "You choose anything you like at the counter. Then we can sit at a table and drink some chocolate or orangeade or anything else. And then you can go back and choose some more cakes. After all, the C.E. comes but once in a lifetime."

"But maybe, Mr. Isaac, we did not pass."

"Fiddlesticks! Of course you did—the three of you! Now don't be polite about those cakes. Just help yourselves to your hearts' content. The only judge is your stomach."

What a treat! They had babas, Napoleons, religieuses, cornets, éclairs, choux à la crème, meringues.

As they were eating, Grandpa Isaac asked, "Who do you think will win the *Tour* this year?" And they were off, talking about the *Tour*. Grandpa Isaac knew so much. "Every year," he said, "I take my delivery truck and go to see the racers as they speed by through the high passes of the Alps."

So they talked, and André feared all the time that his bicycle would be mentioned. But it was not. Neither Michel nor Jack ever brought up the subject. They remembered the strike, so they kept their mouths shut. Solidarity, thought André.

By the time they went back to the hall and Grandpa Isaac had left them they had almost forgotten the C.E. As they waited on the sidewalk for the results, most of the boys looked confident. A few were downhearted.

At last the door opened again and the usher posted the list. The rush was not so great as it had been in the morning because the number of candidates had been greatly reduced. André, Jack, and Michel saw their names right away. Next to Mayer was "Excellent," next to Girard, "Very good," next to Renout, "Good." They saw "Very Good" next to Fausset. Some pupils had "Passing" written beside their names. The two names that were missing were of those boys who had failed the oral part of the examination, and they could try again in October.

It was over! Going home together, André, Jack, and Michel could not believe it. All these years they had worked just for this one day. At long last their first battle with life was won. They had gone through a portal, and their childhood was forever behind them. They had come of age.

They were solemn and a little sad. For this was the parting of the ways. The following day Jack would be leaving for his job as an apprentice in a dam-building project in the southwest. Next October, Michel would follow a Complementary Course in order to enter secondary school later, and so would Fernand. In October, André would enter a technical school. They trudged along thoughtfully. Seven years of close companionship had come to an end.

Suddenly they heard, "Papers! Papers!"

Papers? The *Tour!* The *Tour!* With one accord they started running toward the newsdealer. As they dodged in and out of the crowd, trying to read the headlines and hear the comments, they knew that their hearts would always beat together for that unique, stupendous event: the Big Loop.

VIII. A Single Day

André woke up with a feeling of emptiness. He tried to remember. Yesterday? Ah, yes, he had graduated. His long struggle was over. The night before, Maman had said, "I am proud of you, André. You deserve a good vacation."

Vacation? The little village in Brittany? The sea? The fishing expeditions? Would he again build fortresses, castles, mountains of sand? Was he not too old for that now?

He wondered, and all the time he tried to push away from his mind his one and only thought: his bicycle. He told himself roughly, You knew you could not expect it. So what? But he couldn't help worrying, How long will it be before I get one? Won't it be too late then for me to become a racer?

He got up without enthusiasm. On the table there was a note from Maman, and eighteen francs. The note said, "Here are eighteen francs. Go and get *L'Equipe*. And, at noon, come and fetch me."

Eighteen francs to buy the paper, the sports newspaper! Oh, boy! Quickly he put his head under the faucet, smoothed his hair with his hands, dressed in a jiffy, and tumbled downstairs. When he came back he heated some milk and then sat munching his bread and reading the *Tour* news. What a treat! How did Maman ever think of it?

He read every single line of the paper—that is, all there was about the Big Loop. He did not bother about tennis, boxing, swimming, basketball, and so forth. No. Just the *Tour*. Anyway, three-quarters of the paper was full of it. Titles jumped at one another: MALLEJAC AND LE GUILLY ON THE BRETON TEAM; ANASTESI AND ANQUETIL NEW ADDITIONS TO THE TRICOLORES; LA SQUADRA ARRIVES FROM MILAN; LASTING POPULARITY OF THE BICYCLE IN FRANCE IN SPITE OF MOTORIZING; THE TOUR, THE BIGGEST FRENCH SPORTS EVENT.

And what was this? THE TOUR AND THE AMERICANS. This was a short article saying that the *Tour* was considered by "Americans who are experts at that sort of thing as *a model of efficiency*."

Reading and thinking about the *Tour*, the morning went fast for André. He straightened up the apartment and then he got ready to go to fetch Maman. He folded *L'Equipe* carefully and tucked it in his vest pocket so that just the title would show. Then he was on his way.

He waited across the street from the rear door of the post office. Twelve o'clock. Employees came out, many of them pushing their bicycles in front of them. André looked at them sadly. Maman appeared. She was talking to a man with a racing bicycle. She looked around, and, seeing André, made a sign for him to cross the street. He went over and kissed her, and she said, "And, Mr. Dubois, this is my son, André." They shook hands.

Mr. Dubois smiled. "Well, young man, I hope you will like it. Of course, as I told your mother, it is not new. I cannot guarantee anything, you understand. I don't even know the guy who had it. He is a friend of a friend of a friend. But at that price you cannot expect too much, can you? Well, take it away now, I have to go." And he pushed the handlebar of the bicycle toward André.

"But—but—" stammered André.

Maman said, smiling, "Yes, André, it's yours. Really."

"Ha, ha, ha!" Mr. Dubois laughed. "For a surprise, that *is* surprise! It reminds me of my young days. I was almost fourteen too. My first bike! Did I ride! And look at me now. I can't even go around the block. Bad heart."

"The war, it's the war," Maman commented.

"Right, Madame. The war. So long, Madame. So long, young man. Perhaps you will end up champion of the *Tour* someday. Don't I see *L'Equipe* in your pocket?"

André tried to look casual—as if he had pushed a bike in front of him all his life! But his throat was dry and he could hardly see. Maman trotted beside him, explaining breathlessly, "An unheard-of opportunity! After the strike, as you can imagine, all the savings were gone. So I worked overtime regularly, as you know; not that I ever thought I could make up the sum for the bicycle in that short time, but it was best to start again right away toward the goal. It was while I was working overtime that I met Mr. Dubois. And we began to talk, and before I knew it I had told him about your bicycle. And one day he said he had a friend who knew a friend who had a friend who wanted to get rid of his racing bike, and he would let it go for practically nothing. And that's how it came about. It may be a little hard to control at the beginning because it's a racing bike, but you have grown so fast that I think you will be able to manage it."

André nodded absently. He was not there. This was not real. Somebody else, not he, André, was pushing this bicycle. He walked on like an automaton. He came to as Maman said, "You can leave it downstairs. There is a chain and a padlock. See?"

André did not answer. He just bent over and with one swift movement he swung the bicycle over his shoulder and started up the steps. "I'd rather take it upstairs," he said in a tight voice. "You know, cross-country-race fashion."

They ate, and Maman went back to work. "Be careful," she said, smiling tenderly at him as she closed the door.

He sat there looking at his bicycle lightly resting against the dresser. He still could not believe it. Was it possible to be happier than he was now? He postponed taking his bicycle downstairs, as if the enchantment might vanish. Anyway, he felt that before riding he needed that time of intimate acquaintanceship, there, all alone with it in the quietness of the room. For a long time he did nothing but look at it. Then he got up slowly, ran his hand over the frame, the spokes of the wheels, the pedals, the cranks, the sprockets, the gear shift. At last, when the tumult within him had subsided somewhat, he decided that he would go to Jack's and Michel's to show them, and perhaps they would come out and help him learn how to ride. This was their last chance of being together, since Michel was leaving the next day with Grandpa Isaac, and Jack was going to his new job in the southwest.

He swung the bike on his shoulder and went down. In the street children swarmed around him, chanting excitedly, "André Girard's got a bike! A bike! A bike! Give us a ride, André! Please! Give us a ride!" The children were pressing all around; they were so close that he was afraid they might scratch the lovely new paint, but nevertheless he stopped and picked up a five-year-old boy and put him on the saddle.

"No," said the little boy, "put me on the handlebar and ride with me."

"Little André doesn't know how to ride!" called a contemptuous voice as Fernand swished by on his own bike. André reddened, but the young boy put out his tongue in Fernand's direction and said to André, "I don't care if you can't ride. You put me on your bike. He never did— never. I don't like him. *You* are nice."

"Someday when I know how to ride well I'll take you with me for a real trip around the block. You better let me go now so I can learn."

At the Renouts' he created a sensation. Jack rolled his eyes gaily. "You see, it's this way. I can be pretty sure that with a good job I am going to be able to get my bike in time to train for a professional license. But I couldn't figure out how you could get yours, after the strike and your going for higher education. But now we're all set. And don't think that you will be so far ahead of me that I cannot catch up with you. I can and I will!"

He slapped his strong legs and gave André a friendly push. They laughed. They understood each other. André knew that Jack was right. Jack was older; and besides, though he, André, had suddenly grown very fast, he remained frail-looking and he needed a lot of time in advance for training. Jack did not. So everything was as it should be.

They walked to Michel's. Madame Morel, too, said, "Oh," and "Ah." She promised to tell Michel as soon as he and Grandpa Isaac came back from the oculist's that André and Jack were practicing on the Avenue de l'Observatoire.

When the boys reached their destination André said, "Jack, you try first. You rode last summer. You show me."

"But maybe I won't be able to ride," said Jack, who was already holding the bicycle. "A racing baby—that's different from a sports machine. Such slim wheels! Such a narrow frame!"

"Try anyhow."

"I promise, André, I'll be careful. I won't let her fall."

He swung his leg over the saddle, and off he went, wobbling a little at first; but soon he looked poised and confident. André ran along next to him, but soon Jack was going too fast for him to keep up, so André called, "I'll wait for you here!"

Jack came back, radiant. "Such a different feeling from an ordinary bicycle! So sensitive. It responds to the slightest touch. And she is so fast and light. It feels just as if you were flying. Did you notice the way I sat? The director of the camp said that on a sports or racing bike one should not be hunched; it is bad for the insides. One should adopt the streamlined position discovered by Charles Nieuport."

"By whom?"

"Nieuport. Way back in 1895. He rode on bicycle tracks and thought that one had to be in an almost horizontal position on the bike in order to increase the speed by lessening the air resistance. And this also happens to be the most healthy position for the body when racing. Later, this guy Nieuport got interested in planes, and he started building them streamlined too, see? Now let me hold you. No, don't stand on the pedals. Sit down and hold the handlebars lightly."

Jack gave André a little push and trotted beside him, still holding the saddle. André felt very high and insecure. The front wheel went every which way, so he grabbed the handlebars and pressed down on them with his whole weight.

"Don't! Don't!" cried Jack, trying to steady him. But already André had lost his balance. Instinctively he reached for the ground with his foot, but his fear made him awkward, so he bumped into the revolving pedal. It scraped his ankle and sent him tumbling down sideways with the bicycle on top of him. Jack disengaged him quickly.

André was laughing as he pulled out his handkerchief and tied it around his bleeding ankle. "Did you ever see such a clumsy nitwit?" he asked.

"Oh, I had a couple of falls too," conceded Jack. "That's all in the learning."

"I'll try again right now," said André eagerly. "I know now why it went wrong. It was my putting weight on the handlebars."

He rode again and did much better. Then Jack had a ride. Then André tried with Jack holding him for the start only. Then he did it without any help at all. By the time Michel appeared, André could even turn left and right and apply the brakes.

Michel was just as happy as Jack had been over André's

unexpected good fortune. Right away André said, "You learn too, Michel. We can hold you."

"Wait a minute until I take off my glasses," said Michel.

It did not prove difficult for Michel to get his balance; he was much more relaxed than André. But he did not seem to know where to go. "Watch out!" cried both André and Jack as they saw Michel making straight for the curb. He saved himself from falling only by alighting quickly.

"Can't you *look* where you're going?" Jack exclaimed almost crossly. What Michel had done seemed so stupid.

"That's it," said Michel softly. "I can't."

"Well, put on your glasses," André urged impatiently.

Michel shook his head. "No. I might fall and break them. And they cost a lot of money."

They looked at him, suddenly puzzled and uneasy. Michel was extraordinarily quiet. His face was very calm and his eyes were very brilliant, as if they were full of water.

And all at once André and Jack understood, and with one accord they rushed to him and tried to hug him in spite of his holding the bicycle, saying over and over again, "Oh, you poor old thing!"

Michel said, "It's nothing. No, really. I have known it for so long."

André moaned, "That's just it! And we, all these years, have been talking to you about racing, and the *Tour,* and everything—"

"We are just brutes," Jack declared emphatically. "Just brutes!"

"It's my fault," said Michel. "I should have told you. But I couldn't bear to. Remember last year when you asked me if I wanted to be a racer?"

"Yes, you laughed kind of queerly," said André.

"I remember," said Jack, "You were awfully cagey about the whole thing."

Michel sighed. "I wanted to fool myself as long as I could."

"I know," said André. And he did. He too had wanted to keep hoping. Only for him there had been a sort of miracle, whereas for Michel there never could be any miracle. Michel would never be a racer. It seemed bitter that Michel was denied what he wanted most and what had made their friendship so close. Silent and distraught, they stood near the bike.

Michel was the first to recover. He pulled out his handkerchief and wiped his glasses carefully. He wiped his eyes too. Then he put on his glasses, raised his head, smiled, and yelled, " 'Against us they were hundreds of thousands, and in command were kings!' " He gave Jack and André a big slap. *"Sambre et Meuse! Sambre et Meuse!* Go on, get your practicing in! There is not much time."

Indeed, they felt they should make the most of their last day together. André and Jack took turns riding, while Michel kept the other one company. By the end of the afternoon André had no fear left, and they all agreed that in his next turn, when he would be on his own entirely, he could try some traffic lights on the gentle incline of the Boulevard Raspail.

When they finally said good-by at André's door it did not seem like a real parting, so excited were they about the bike. Each one said, "I'll write you," though no one was sure he would do it. They really meant, "I won't forget you," and that was the truth.

André rode all by himself the next morning, and by noon he felt like a veteran on the bike. Not only could he stop gradually, but he could go downhill safely and he was not afraid of the traffic. What a wonderful vacation he was going to have! And even after school opened he could keep practicing and gradually get into shape.

He had two years ahead of him to run in amateur races until he could get his professional license (the *Fédération Française du Cyclisme* does not give racing licenses to boys until they are sixteen years of age). Then, under careful supervision, he could start building up his endurance, developing his style, and acquiring a reputation. Many a secondary but difficult professional race has to be won before the *Tour* can be tackled. André knew that so far no champion under twenty years of age had ever won the *Tour*. Could he? Anyway, he needed all that time ahead of him, every bit of it, because he was not built like Jack or Fernand. And Fernand had already been riding for the last six months. Oh, well, now he, André, was on his way.

Leisurely he turned to go home for lunch. He pedaled

along the Boulevard St. Michel, waited at the intersection for the light, and took Soufflot Street going up toward the Panthéon. Just for fun he decided to go up the slight hill *en danseuse*—like a dancer—which is the technical term, employed by racers, meaning the lifting of oneself off the saddle, and, body almost vertical, pushing the pedals down. This gives the whole body a swaying movement; hence the expression *monter en danseuse*—to go up like a dancer. Some racers like it for a steep hill, others don't. André tried it, anyway, and he could not help wondering if people were looking at him. But they were not; there were too many other bicycles, motorcycles, motorbikes, scooters, cars, and buses on the street. No one paid any attention to a slim, lanky boy going up a hill *en danseuse*. But someday . . . someday . . .

And now, what about going down La Mouff'? That would be quite something: negotiating the hilly, narrow, crowded street; and besides, André wanted to show the children how well he could ride. The worst that could happen would be that he would have to get off.

He crossed the Place de la Contrescarpe and cautiously started down Mouffetard Street. It had rained during the night, and the tramping of so many feet had prevented the pavement from drying properly. He wormed his way slowly among the stands and the people shopping. Children shrieked, "Look, it's André! Look at him! How well he rides!" And some older people said, "Careful, careful, my boy. Goodness, he already looks like a racer."

Suddenly somebody darted right in front of him,

shouting at the same time, "Your rear wheel is bent!"
Fernand!

Abruptly André swerved in order to avoid him, barely
missing him and feeling all rattled at the false warning.
And the next thing he knew, straight ahead was a broken
strip of pavement. It was too late to go around it. His front
wheel went down, smack, in the little ditch. The impact
threw André off his bicycle, down on the slimy pavement;
and a sound like splitting wood rent the air.

He was up almost at once, pushing quickly through the
crowd around him to get to his bike, which lay a few
yards away. He raised it gently, and it fell apart: the
front fork had snapped, the frame was broken in several
pieces.

He stood there speechless. He could not believe it.
This was just a nightmare. People gathered around him,
asking, "Are you hurt?" He did not know and did not
care. Men crowded around the bicycle. Shaking their
heads sadly, they bent to examine the pieces.

One of the men suddenly swore and said, "Look! If
that isn't the dirtiest deal you ever saw! Who sold you
that bike, my boy? Whoever did is a crook. That bike was
broken before, and it was just put back together and
glued and painted over. See the break marks? They are
old. You were lucky that it didn't fall apart on a hill at
forty miles an hour. It's sheer murder to have sold you
such a thing. Should be in jail, that guy. You go back to
him and tell him to give you another machine. This one
is done for completely. Tell him you'll sue!"

Sue! André picked up the pieces of the lamentable trophy, walked up the few steps at the entrance to his apartment house, went up the stairs and into the flat, put the bike in a heap in a corner, and sat down. When Maman came in he had his head hidden in his arms on the table. Uncontrollable sobs shook him.

As Maman was going back to work she said, "I'll tell Mr. Dubois right away. He was not at the post office this morning, but I'll surely see him this afternoon. After all, one cannot be cheated to that extent."

André, seated in front of his untouched plate, looked at her sadly. "Don't you remember that Mr. Dubois doesn't know the name of the man—that he is a friend of a friend of a friend? And that Mr. Dubois said that he couldn't guarantee anything?"

"He meant that he could not guarantee that the bicycle would run for many years," Maman said hotly, "not that it would not fall apart at once. And besides, this is criminal."

"But Mr. Dubois can't do anything, since he doesn't know the man."

"Can't do anything, indeed! He can trace the crook!"

"And then what?"

"I tell you, André, Mr. Dubois will help us. Cheer up. I'll see him this afternoon."

He knew Maman wanted him to feel better. She had made the deal and felt responsible, though of course no one could possibly have detected the flaw. The man in the street had said it was bound to happen. If only it had not happened so soon! It was Fernand's fault. Yes, it was. André had been so upset that he had not seen the ditch in time. And the rear wheel was *not* bent. That was a lie. He tightened his fists. But suppose it had happened later, the splitting of the rotten frame on a hill—at forty miles an hour.

Now nothing could be done. The bicycle was beyond repair. Maman said Mr. Dubois would help. But André knew better. It was all over. He had had one single glorious day.

He continued to sit at the table, numb with grief. Time went on, and he never realized that the afternoon had passed and his full lunch plate was still in front of him. The sun was going down, and soon Maman would be back. He had no hope, and yet as the hour approached he became fidgety and anxious. He got up and started to pace the floor. The moment Maman opened the door he knew the answer from the look on her face. But what she said he could not possibly have expected.

"Mr. Dubois—died—this morning. Heart attack. We heard the news this afternoon."

IX. Kicking Over the Traces

He could not sleep. His bicycle, the *Tour*—all his hopes shattered within a second. Twenty-four hours of utter bliss, free to move and go places under his own power, and with the prospect of gradually getting into shape for his life's ambition. One single day. And now he was back where he had been before. The *Tour* had receded into an impossible future, and he was again a young, dependent boy, closed in, hemmed in on all sides, in his mother's apartment. He choked up.

He thought of Michel, bereft of both father and mother; Michel, whose heart, too, was set on a bike and the *Tour*— and yet he could never, never so much as hope to become a racer. But Michel did not buckle under. Yes, but as far as cycling was concerned, Michel was up against a natural disability. It was hard, but it couldn't be helped; whereas he, André—

But what about Jack? He too had the same dream, and his family could not help him toward it. No, but Jack was doing something about it himself. Right now he was on his way to his job. He would make money and save to buy his bicycle. Whereas André could do nothing but grin and bear it, like a good little boy. "Little André," "shriveled shrimp," "little runt." He tossed around and bit his lips in the dark. He could not vindicate his own name. Fernand would be a racer before he even got started. Fernand would win the *Tour*. And he, Girard's son— Burning tears fell on his cheeks.

But, after all, suppose he had never had a bike? There *had* been the strike, and he hadn't been expecting a bike after that—or had he? Well, couldn't he just imagine that he'd never had one? But he *had*! He *had*! And he couldn't forget it.

Next evening when Maman came back from work she was surprised not to find André home. As time went on she grew more and more anxious. When he staggered in, two hours later, she gasped. He was grim and wan; his mouth was set and his eyes hard; his clothes were rumpled and his hands black. He looked older.

"I am working!" he cried defiantly.

"Working!" Maman collapsed on a chair. Working! Where? Why? For how long? What about vacation? What about school? Working! At fourteen! Oh no, no, this could not be!

For hours they argued. He felt he was hurting her terribly. He wished he could find the right words to soothe her. But he only knew what he wanted.

Finally the fierce discussion came to an end, as Maman started to cry. All at once André's harshness left him, and he came over to her and put his arm around her shoulders, pleading softly, "Maman, don't, I beg you. There is nothing you can do about it—nothing. I want a bike as soon as possible. I want to become a professional racer like my father. So I am going to work."

And from then on he did.

He was up every morning at five-thirty. Maman was up too, no matter what her schedule was. In silence he would gulp down the coffee she had prepared. It was meant to give him some pep for the long day ahead. He needed it. His was not healthy work in the open, like a farmboy's. It was factory work, in a plant manufacturing plane parts.

At five minutes past six he would snatch the lunchbag Maman had packed for him, sling it over his shoulder, and, still in silence, reach for his beret. Then, before putting it on, he would kiss Maman good-by. He wished he did not have to. But it was too much of a French tradition to by-pass, even when bitter disagreement smoldered between them, as it did now. Then he would race downstairs and make for the subway, together with a crowd of working people. Forty minutes on the subway, then a ten-minute walk, and just before the seven-o'clock whistle he punched the clock at the plant. And he was indoors until six o'clock at night, except for an hour and a half interruption for lunch.

He had to stand all day long on the same spot before a conveyer belt. The belt rolled like a mechanical carpet, endlessly, and on it identical machine parts traveled, all evenly spaced, and in so doing came in front of André, each one in turn. He had to do the same thing to every part. Hour after hour he would make the same motions. The conveyer belt moved on and on rhythmically. Its speed was too fast for young and unskilled André, and the strain on him was very great. His body ached and his spirit became numb after a few hours of work.

Back home at night, if Maman was home, dinner would be ready. Otherwise he would warm up whatever she had left and eat alone. Then he wanted nothing but to creep into bed.

But he always remembered that a racer should be scrupulously clean. So he would make the tremendous effort of heating some water and washing himself from head to foot and brushing his teeth. At last, exhausted, he would tumble into bed, having previously opened his window wide. He would mumble to himself, "Early to bed, up early, sleep with plenty of fresh air, like a racer . . . like a racer . . . like . . . a . . . rac . . ." And then it would be five-thirty and the smell of coffee was filling the room.

Every day was the same, except Sunday—and Saturday, because it was summer. On the first Saturday he was miserable. He had a cold and was running a fever. He could see in Maman's eyes what she was thinking, though she did not say anything. But if she hoped that he would quit, she was mistaken. Oh no! Wasn't he training to be a racer? And what does a racer do who has a cold? He stays in bed, bundles up warmly and drinks quarts and quarts of lemonade and linden tea, and sweats the cold out, does he not?

He was back at work on Monday.

When the second Saturday came around he felt exhausted and very blue. It was not only the work that was killing him. The fact that the men were unfriendly and that he didn't know what to do about it added an intolerable weight to his misery. How long would he be able to stand it? How long would it be before he could buy his own bike? He ached all over, in body and heart.

That day there was a letter from Michel.

My old André,

Mother wrote me about your bike. How ghastly! I can hardly believe it. What are you going to do? I told Grandpa Isaac about it all and he said right away, "Why don't you ask André to come here and spend the summer with us? It won't cost him more than to go to Brittany by train, and I would rather have two boys than one, anyway."

So what do you say, André? Please do come quickly. I'll be so happy.

My respects to your mother.

Yours,
Michel

Good old Grandpa Isaac! Just like him! And Michel too, for that matter. Well, that was some offer. Two months away from the city, in the fresh mountain air and in Michel's and Grandpa Isaac's company. Wonderful!

Whistling happily, he grabbed his pen and a piece of paper.

My old Michel,

You are a brick, and so is Grandpa Isaac! I cannot tell you how thankful I am. Is it all right if I come

He paused. Was he giving up? Was he a quitter? No. He had gone to work. He had proved he was no weakling. He would stop working on Maman's account. Yes, that was it. Maman was too unhappy. He would go to Grandpa Isaac's now. She would be so pleased. Later, if he wished, he could always resume working, couldn't he? He got up to look at the calendar, the regular post-office calendar that the postman brought as a present every New Year's. He would go a week from tomorrow. That would give Michel time to answer him about meeting him at the station and everything. Oh, boy! Oh, boy! He felt that he was with Michel and Grandpa Isaac already, and the factory but a past nightmare.

He came back to the table, and as he sat down he noticed, in the lower right-hand corner of Michel's letter the letters T.S.V.P., meaning, "Turn, please." He did, and read, "Do you think Hassendorfer will win?"

He blushed to the roots of his hair. The *Tour!* The

Tour! Fiercely he tore up the letter he had started to write and began all over again.

My old Michel,

You are a brick, and so is Grandpa Isaac. I cannot thank you enough. But I cannot accept. I have gone to work. I am earning money toward my bike . . .

When he finished the letter he felt collected and determined. As he sealed the envelope he suddenly knew what he was going to do with his free day. He was going to train. Train? He had no bike. But what could prevent him from walking?

He went out at a brisk, steady pace, crossed St. Michel's bridge, cut through back streets, and went up the Grands Boulevards. And there was the office of the *Parisien Libéré,* where he could read the news of the *Tour* on the paper posted outside.

A group of men were crowded around the window. He listened to their comments while reading the paper.

"That Alsatian, Hassendorfer, a daredevil!"

"Beginner's luck."

"He won't stomach the mountains."

"Duplay has broken down on the easy Riviera stretch!"

"Can you beat that?"

"Well, he had it coming to him."

"Sure! You've got to be awfully strict with yourself when you're professional, especially if you want to run in the Big Loop. Some guys can take the running, all right, but they can't take the personal discipline and sooner or later they break down."

Everybody agreed, and André nodded knowingly. Someday, perhaps, these same men would again be looking at the paper, and the headline would read "girard." And they would never know that he had been right among them that day, when he was earning money for his bike and had already begun his training: going to bed early, sleeping with his window open, not smoking, keeping clean, washing his teeth, clipping his toenails, eating as much fruit and vegetables as he could persuade his mother to buy, and taking vigorous walks whenever he could.

Right now he had better not loiter any more, but go back at a clipped and rhythmical pace. He would get home in time for lunch. He took large avenues so that he could exercise better—the Avenue de l'Opéra, through the Tuileries Gardens, along the Seine, and up the Boulevard St. Michel. Then, as he turned the corner of Soufflot Street, whom did he see coming the other way but Mr. Valeur!

He raised his beret and was just going by, but Mr. Valeur came over to him, stopped, and shook hands, saying, "I heard that you have gone to work, André. It is all right for vacation time, but you are not going to keep it up, are you? One does not throw away chances for a better education."

"I know, sir. But you see, I want to buy myself a bike."

"Think it over, André, think it over. You are quick-tempered and you also have the passionate temperament of the Breton: everything or nothing. On the other hand, you also have the Breton ability to carry through against wind and tide and to accomplish, by sheer stubborn per-severance, whatever your heart is set on. So don't make the wrong choice. If you have to go on working now, do it; but before school starts, will you come and talk it over with me?"

"Why, yes, sir."

"Promise?"

"Promise."

"Good. Speaking of bicycles, did you hear that Duplay broke down? That chap had been all right so far. Then he made a little money on the racing tracks, and it spoiled him. He went in for rich food, smoking, late hours."

"He will have an awful time getting himself back in shape," remarked André.

"Yes, if he ever does. It takes backbone to run the *Tour*, not only muscles. I bet the Tricolores are mad. A guy who runs wild ruins a team's chances. You just can't let yourself go like that. You've got to think of the others. Remember? Jack used to call it solidarity."

"Yes, I remember," André said, smiling as he recalled that day in Mr. Valeur's class.

"And, by the way, I heard that Jack has gone to work too."

"Yes, he had to. But he is going to save all the money he can to buy his bike."

"I see. And you are going to do the same, even though you won a scholarship for technical school? Well, as I said, think it over, and come see me in September. This is a friendly invitation. You know where I live, don't you? So long. My respects to your mother."

They shook hands and parted. Good old Valeur! Wonderful fellow. He had a way of speaking to you as if you were his equal. It made André feel he could accomplish anything. Of course he would not quit working when school reopened. Whatever happened at the factory, he would stick through thick and thin. Then he would go to see old Valeur. The teacher had invited him. "This is a friendly invitation." Well, that was something! André did not know of any boy in his class who had actually stepped into Mr. Valeur's apartment. So he would call on old Valeur, but he would not tell Maman about it beforehand, for fear she would entertain false hopes. The sooner she realized it, the better: there was no turning back; he was going to be a racer, like his father, and run in the *Tour*.

X. The Years Between

"So," said Mr. Valeur, "you don't want to go back to school. All right. Then, will you let me coach you?"

"What for, sir?"

"Because, as I have often told you and the other boys in my classes, it does not hurt a racer to know something besides cycling. In fact, it helps him out. Nowadays champs meet important people; they are interviewed by reporters; they speak over the radio. Soon they will appear on television. You don't want to look and act as if you were straight from the backwoods, do you? You've got to travel not only the roads of the country, but also the roads of the mind—some of them, at least."

"Like what, sir?"

"Well, first of all, you need a foreign language. And

you have to learn it so you can speak it. French racers run in England. Dutch and Australian racers come over here and they speak English. Someday you might run in the six-day bicycle race in New York, at Madison Square Garden. You don't want to be shut in within yourself. You want to talk to people. With English and French at your command, you can get along pretty well. So, what about learning English?"

"All right. I think I would like it."

"Good. Now, what about some history? That wouldn't hurt either, would it?"

"To tell you the truth, sir, I don't think I would care for it. All about wars, conquests, and politics."

"But what I mean is the history of civilization, the inventions of men—the wheel, steam power, electricity, atomic energy—and the literary and artistic creations of men; and the beautiful ideas to which some men consecrated their lives; and also the great inner vision for which some of them were willing to die. That's what our world is made of, and everybody, including a cyclist, has a right to know about it."

"Is that history?"

"What else?"

"Well, it doesn't sound like what I expected. Only, sir, I am afraid if I learn all that, it will make me different from my fellow workers at the plant." He did not want to tell Mr. Valeur that already he was not on good terms with the men at the factory.

"Right you are!" exclaimed Mr. Valeur. "Don't you ever

let yourself be cut off from them. You would not be any good as a racer then, either. Who is crazy about the *Tour de France?* It is not the rich, or the snobs, or the highbrows. It is the people, the working people and the artists and writers. The *Tour* is truly the child of the people, and because of this it is also the child of peace."

André nodded. "When there is a war, there is no *Tour.*"

"Correct. People, peace, and the *Tour*—they always go together. Now, coming back to your being different: when you learn about working conditions through the ages, the tools used by people, their struggles and their dreams, can't you see that you are going to feel much closer to your fellow workers in the plant?"

"Do you think so?" André asked hopefully.

"Surely. And that will make a better man of you. It will help the racer in you too."

André hesitated. "Sir, how much would the lessons cost?"

"Oh that! Forget it."

"Oh, no, sir, I couldn't. It is work to give me lessons, and work has to be paid for. Any kind of work."

"All right, André. Then what about helping me with the correcting of my class papers in mathematics? You are good at it. That will save me time and labor."

It was a deal, and André left Mr. Valeur in better spirits than he had come. Mr. Valeur seemed to take it for granted that he would be a racer—and in the *Tour*. It was always as if Mr. Valeur had never been aware of André's handicaps, physical or financial.

Michel turned up a few weeks later. He was in a Complementary Course and had so much homework that he had no free time whatever. "What's new?" he asked. "Have you heard from Jack?"

"No. He doesn't write."

"What about going to the Renouts' now to find out about him?"

Arm in arm they went down La Mouff'. Michel said slowly, "Fernand is in my class."

"Ah. Still riding his sports bike?"

"Nope. He's got a racing model now."

"A racing model!" André gasped.

"Yes. And he's so smart with his homework that he manages to train regularly. He is already talking about amateur races."

"Oh no, it can't be." André groaned. "He will be way ahead of me long before I make so much as a start."

They knocked at the door of the Renouts' apartment.

"Lambkins!" exclaimed Mrs. Renout, kissing both of them affectionately. "Come in! And how is my White Rabbit André faring?"

"White Rabbit, my eye!" thundered Mr. Renout. "He is a working man now!" And he shook hands and slapped André on the shoulder. "Just had a letter from our Jack this morning. He is not much for writing, you know. Never was smart like you, Michel. But he is doing fine. He has had a small raise in salary. It's a good project down there."

Mrs. Renout sighed. "Yes, it is a good project, all right.

But I wish just the same he hadn't had to start working so early—and go so far, in addition."

"Well, my Big One, that's life! No bed of roses for poor people. But our Jack will make it somehow, I trust. Ah, while I think of it, he writes something which is going to interest both you boys, André especially. Jack is boarding with a family, of course, and the boy there—"

"Papa!" yelled Miquette. "Don't! Don't, Papa!"

But it was too late. Mr. Renout had already said, "—has a bicycle."

"How could you? How could you?" wailed Miquette.

"Shut up!" Mrs. Renout ordered Miquette. She turned to her husband, scowling, her fists on her hips. "Alphonse, you are just so smart that it hurts!"

Mr. Renout looked sheepish for a moment; then he brought his fist down on the table. "What's all this ruckus about? Maybe I spoke out of turn, but André was bound to know it sooner or later, wasn't he? And he can take it, can't you, André?"

André squared his thin shoulders and swallowed hard. "Yes, sir. Of course. Mighty glad for Jack, if he can practice."

"That's the spirit!" roared Mr. Renout. "And don't you worry, my boy, your turn will come too."

Back in the street, Michel and André did not speak. After walking for a while, Michel said quietly, "It's tough. I know."

André did not answer. He was grateful to Michel for

not trying to cheer him up. It was useless to delude himself: he was left behind—behind Fernand, behind Jack. All the luck was against him. Maybe he had chosen wrong; maybe he could never be a racer.

Michel quoted, as if talking to himself, " 'One should put up with discouragement, and after a fall get up again.' "

André tried to smile as he shook hands to say good-by. "Thanks, Old One. It's a good line, especially for a racer."

His heart was heavy. If only things had been right at the factory. But they were not. That's what he could not explain to Mr. Valeur, or to anybody. He kept hoping the situation would change. But, far from improving, it was getting worse and worse. It had got off to a wrong start months before, at the beginning, at the very first lunch.

Those workers who did not go home for the meal got together to eat, and André had joined them. The men had offered him a smoke and a drink of wine. He had said, "No, thank you." At first they thought it was because he was shy, and they urged him. "Don't be bashful—take it!" But as days and weeks passed, and he always refused, they started jeering at him. "What's the matter with you? Are you sick? Got to be a man! What's wrong?" And then they went further. "High-hat, eh? We fellows are not good enough for you!"

If only he could have said, "I cannot smoke and I cannot drink because I am going to be a racer." Then everything would have been simple. But he couldn't bring himself to say it. He was afraid the men would ridicule him, as Fernand always had. It was true that he was tall by now, but he was still lean. "Breadless Day," a man had called him once. And, above all, he had no bicycle. What kind of future racer was he, anyhow? So he bit his lips, bent his stubborn head, and remained silent. And the men continued to jeer at him all the more. Once he even thought he heard something like "dirty Breton head." When the men were in a good mood they took to calling him "the Character"—"How is the Character?" "Don't offer a cigarette to the Character," and so on. Sometimes he felt he could not stand it much longer. And still he held on.

When André arrived at the plant one Monday he found another boy at the conveyer belt. His heart sank. Was he dismissed? The foreman came around and said, "Girard, come this way. You have been promoted. From now on you will work at a machine tool; and you get a raise of three hundred francs a week."

He was jubilant—until lunchtime. When he joined the group he quickly saw the faces around him were like a stone wall. When lunch was over and the men went back to work, he caught bits of phrases: "The Character . . . ," "Dirty kid . . . ," "Fawning around the foreman . . . ," "Sly, quiet type . . . ," "Underhanded . . . ," "Unreliable . . ."

He was indignant. He had never so much as spoken to the foreman! But how was he going to convince them? They were ready to believe anything against him because he was different. If he could only explain, "I want to be a racer." But just the thought of uttering those words choked him.

The rest of the week was a nightmare, so much so that when Sunday came he failed to get ready for his usual walking exercise. What was the use? Maman looked at him thoughtfully. She did not ask any questions, but suggested that they take a walk together in the afternoon. He agreed in a listless sort of way.

It was a leisurely walk, not one for training. On their way home, as they passed a café terrace, they heard people talking in shrill voices. There was an elderly couple, arguing with the waiter. They yelled at the tops of their voices, and the more they did, the less the waiter could make out what they wanted, because they spoke English. They seemed to expect that if they talked loudly enough in English the French waiter would finally understand. Before he knew what he was doing, André had stopped and asked slowly, "Excuse me. May I help you?"

"He speaks English!" the man cried happily. "Molly, he speaks English!"

"Molly" smiled at André in the friendliest fashion. André said hastily, "I speak a little." And at the same time he tried wildly to remember all he had learned from Mr. Valeur during the past months. The gentleman explained what he and his wife wanted, and André translated it to the waiter. Then, when all was clear, André bowed and said good-by.

But the woman said, "No, no, have a drink with us."

Maman asked André what the lady had said, and when he told her she shook her head energetically, saying to André, "The idea! We don't even know them! We have never seen them before!" Then she said to the couple in French, *"Merci bien, M'sieu. Merci, Madame."* and started to go away.

But the man called to André, "Wait a minute, please! My wife and I are alone. We are lonely." Then he looked at Maman, and said haltingly, *"S'il—vous—plaît, Madame."* Well, Maman could not resist that. She smiled graciously and sat down with them, saying firmly to André, at the same time, "And don't you let them pay for our drinks!" Then she relaxed happily; she really was curious to see how much English André knew.

The conversation was not easy; it all went very slowly. André understood fairly well, but speaking was difficult. Mr. and Mrs. Williams were traveling. They lived in Yellow Springs, Ohio. They thought France was beautiful, and they liked French food. That reminded André of American children eating butter and jam on their square pieces of bread, and he managed to ask about this. They laughed, and told him it was true—and why not? Well, it was too hard to explain to them why not, so he let it go. He asked them whether American boys had bicycles.

"Sure!" said Mr. Williams. "Even little tots have them."

André frowned. Tots? He did not know the word. Mrs. Williams made a gesture of raising her hand from the floor. André gasped. What a country! But then he thought

quickly that she must be referring to toys. Toys! That
was not what he had in mind! So he asked, "Big men,
bicycles?"

Mr. Williams shook his head. "No. In America men
have cars, automobiles. One person out of three has a
car."

André said, "In France one person out of four has a
bicycle."

"Do you have one?" Mrs. Williams asked.

"No, but I will. I am saving my money. I want to—"

And then he got stuck, because he did not know the
word "racer" in English. So he made his legs move, faster
and faster, as if he were pedaling, and he bent forward
as if holding the handlebars; and the Williamses laughed
and said, "Ah, you want to go fast, is that it?"

Well, that was not it at all. And how could he make
them understand? He asked, "Do you know about the
Tour of France?"

"Oh, yes!" Mrs. Williams beamed. "We do it!"

André almost burst out laughing. Of course she had
misunderstood him. After all, anybody touring around
France, just visiting, was making a tour of France. How
could he explain what he meant—that it was a technical
term, a sports term? Ah, there it was! Sports!

"No," he said, "the *Tour de France*—a sport—big
sports event." He pulled a pencil from his pocket, and on
the marble of the café table he drew a map of France and
the line of a circuit going through certain towns. Then he

said, "See? Every year. In July. Twenty-seven days. Three thousand miles. Competition. Huge, huge sport. Everybody in France is excited!"

"My word," exclaimed Mr. Williams, "this sounds fascinating! Tell us some more about it."

Now that the Williamses had some idea of what André was talking about they could help him out with the words he didn't know, and by and by he told them a lot about the *Tour.* Mr. Williams said over and over again, "Just like the World Series back home. And to think that we did not know about it!"

André said, "*I* know about the World Series in the United States. Why don't *you* know about the *Tour de France?* What do they teach you in America about French people?"

Mr. Williams chortled and said, "They teach us about the Reds."

"The Reds!" exclaimed André, all puzzled. "But they live in America!"

Mr. and Mrs. Williams laughed so hard that Maman asked André what it was all about. He said, "I don't know. Something I don't get. He says they teach in America that there are Reds in France. But it doesn't make sense, because Indians are Americans."

"Excuse us for laughing," Mr. Williams said. "We aren't laughing at you. It's just a joke—too hard to explain. But we are so happy to know about the *Tour de France.* Sorry to have missed it this year. We have to go back to America next week. When are you going to race?

Don't you have to train for several years before you can compete professionally?"

So they spoke about training, and Mrs. Williams shook her head sadly toward Maman when she heard that André not only had no bicycle, but that he had to work in a factory to get one.

Mr. Williams said, "You've got pluck, my boy."

"Pluck?"

"Yes, pluck, courage, will power, determination. You will get there. And when you do, let us know. I am going to give you our address in America, and you write to us. And when you race in the *Tour*, we will come to see you if we are still alive."

"All the way from America?" asked André, wide-eyed.

"Of course. Why not?"

André beamed. There was something strong and healthy and daring and confident in the way Mr. Williams spoke. He made everything sound possible. "Why not?" Those two cheery little words came back over and over again.

André called the waiter so that he could pay for his drink and his mother's. But Mr. Williams wouldn't let him. So André finally rose and shook hands and said, "Thank you very much. My turn later: champagne when I am a champ!" And he was quite pleased with his play on words. Maman, too, seemed almost gay for the first time since he had gone to work. She had been very proud of his carrying on a conversation in English.

Monday did not seem half as bad as usual. There was a

small song in his heart, and the refrain was, "Why not?" Then, in the middle of the morning, there was confusion in the shop: the boy who had replaced André at the conveyer belt had fainted.

At lunchtime André was presented by the men with a sheet of paper to sign. It was a petition asking the management not to put fourteen-year-old boys at that conveyer belt. Promptly André got out his pencil; hadn't he himself suffered bitterly from that fast rhythm?

Then one of the men said coldly, "Perhaps the Character does not know that he is sticking his neck out. Everybody who signs this petition is in danger of losing his job."

André looked up quickly. "I know," he said. "It has always been that way, right down through history. Some people have had to stick their necks out in order to get better working conditions." And without a moment's hesitation he signed the sheet and gave it back, saying, "Solidarity."

There was a silence around him. The men eyed him curiously. Then they looked at one another, and it was as if they were about to say something, something nice. But they did not; and after a while they just dispersed quietly.

A week later the management agreed: no fourteen-year-old boy at that conveyer belt any more. Pierre, the young apprentice who had fainted, came to shake hands with André. "If *you* had not signed, you who had just worked at that belt, the management would not have come through."

André felt happy, and he wished that Pierre did not go home to lunch every day. Yet for some reason he did not dread that time so much any more. Lately there had been a sort of relaxation in the atmosphere, and he was not teased any more. He wondered why. Perhaps it was because the *Tour* had started and everybody had his mind on it.

That particular day as he listened to the men discussing while they ate, he heard one of them say, "It's not enough to have muscles and courage. You've got to train properly. And that doesn't mean only to be able to 'knit' fast. You've got to live the right kind of life, and start doing it, mind you, way back, years before you actually race, when you're still a kid."

André nodded, and suddenly he heard his own voice saying, "Yes, I know. *I* want to race in the *Tour* someday."

The men stopped eating and looked at him, thunderstruck. And all at once they started to laugh and they got up and slapped him on the back and said, "Why didn't you say so sooner? Why didn't you talk? Why didn't you? All the time we kept wondering what was the matter with you, acting so different and all that!" They looked at one another and called gaily, "So the kid wants to run in the *Tour!*"

One of them said, "Didn't I always tell you that the kid was okay? No double-crosser? And didn't he sign the petition?"

"And not only that," said another man, "but he talked

well at the time too, like someone who knows what it's all about, and yet he is awfully young."

André smiled. There it was, just as Mr. Valeur had told him: his knowledge of history had brought him closer to his fellow workers.

The men chanted, "Right, right! And he is in dead earnest about the *Tour* too. No mistake! Even stood up against all of us, in his quiet way, all this time: no smoking, no drinking. Well now, André, it's like this—"

And they started giving him all sorts of advice on what he should do and what he should not do and the way to handle his bike. He said, "Yes, yes." Of course he wouldn't let them know that he didn't have a bicycle. Everything was going so beautifully that he was not going to spoil it. But all of a sudden a North African fellow said softly, "Maybe you no bike?"

And André reddened so much that the men knew at once. "What!" they cried. "We are a bunch of idiots! Takes a North African to figure out a Breton! The kid hasn't even got a bike!"

André got up and said nonchalantly, as he did not want them to pity him, "I'll get a bike."

One man said, "Yes, you will, my boy. You've got guts. Only don't keep to yourself so much. Talk a bit once in a while. It helps."

"Leave him alone," said another one. "He is a Breton. They don't gabble, but, believe me, they deliver the goods. The *Tour* is full of Bretons."

"That's right," said someone else. "Bobet, Le Guilly,

Mallejac—not forgetting that phenomenal fellow who was the greatest hope of the French team before the war. Remember? What was his name?"

"Gir— My word!" shouted another man. "Girard! That was his name. Any relative of yours, by any chance, kid?"

"He was my father."

"Thousands of thousands of thunders! Here we've had among us Girard's son, and we— Fools, triple idiots! Well, look here, André, go right on with your training: no smoking, no drinking, plenty of fruit and fresh green vegetables, early to bed with an open window, keep clean, brush your teeth, and clip your toenails carefully —everything that someone who wants to become a racer should do, bike or no bike. You've got to build yourself up, see? From now on we're all solidly behind you."

"You've got to build yourself up." That meant they thought it could be done, that he was not hopelessly unfit physically.

From that day on, André went to work every morning feeling light-hearted. And he looked forward to the lunch period. Also, he came to love quitting time, when they all went to the subway station together and talked of bicycles and the *Tour.*

One evening as he stepped out of the gate with the group of men, there was Michel waiting for him. André's heart sank. Michel looked so spotless, you could tell at once that he was not a factory worker. Maybe this was going to make André unpopular all over again.

But he needn't have worried. One minute after they all started walking together, Michel was like one of them. And he was asking smart questions about the factory and working and living conditions. The men were telling him how hard it was for a worker's family to find living quarters.

Then Michel turned to the North African and said suddenly, "I'll bet you have no place to sleep."

The North African smiled his gentle smile and said, "Maybe you journalist?"

"I'll be darned!" exclaimed Michel. "That's just what I want to be! Look, here is an address. The people are rag-pickers. You go there, and maybe they can find a roof for you during the winter."

The walk to the subway seemed too short, especially after they had started talking about the *Tour*. The men shook hands with Michel and said, "Come again! You'll make a good journalist, you know how to make people talk!" They added, laughing, "Not like André here! He has an ox on his tongue!"

And one of them playfully pulled André's ear. "Don't go on thinking, my boy, that you are the only one who can keep quiet."

"What did he mean?" Michel asked as he and André ran down the subway steps.

"Don't know. Nothing. Just talk, I guess. Michel, I'm so glad you came. You made a hit, honest you did. What's new?"

"Something you won't like. Fernand has quit school.

He is going to do nothing but train. His uncle is financing him."

That was indeed bad news, and André was still brooding over it when on a Saturday night, while waiting his turn at the baker's, he heard a reproachful voice. "So you don't even say hello."

Miquette! He blushed as Miquette went on, "You never come around any more."

"I guess I don't have the time."

"It's not that at all. It's because Papa told you about Jack's having a chance to practice on a bike, that's what it is!"

André made a great effort and asked, "How is he doing?"

"Not bad."

"Is he going out every day?"

Miquette shrugged her shoulders as if she didn't know and said quickly, "He always asks about you in his letters —that is, when he writes. He's not much good at it, you know."

"He's like me. Besides, I wouldn't have anything to tell."

Miquette looked sad. "I know. I wish I could do something. It's so tough, your being without a bike."

He said firmly, "Thanks, Miquette. But don't you worry. I'll get there all right."

"Oh, you're wonderful, André," said Miquette as she shook hands. Then, with eyes full of admiration, she watched André cross the street, head held high.

"I'll get there all right." So he had said proudly. He didn't want Miquette to pity him. But in his heart he had almost ceased to believe it. The pull was too long. There were too many odds against him.

Next day on his way to the plant, he was gloomy. Not even the saint's-day card from Maman that he had found on his breakfast plate could warm his spirit. He went to his locker in a sort of mechanical, absent-minded way, and practically stumbled on a shining bicycle that was parked in front of the row of lockers. He started to move it, and his eyes bulged. The contraption was tied with a ribbon to his own locker! And then he saw the card on the handlebars: *Vive la Saint-André!* He turned white and steadied himself against the locker.

The men rushed to him. "Eh there, kid! This is no time to pass out, now that Saint André sends you a present— straight from heaven!" They teased him good-humoredly, all the more so because most of them were not religious at all. "Some guy, that fellow Saint André! Right smart!"

Well, bit by bit, it all finally came out. Everyone in the lunch group had had a hand in that bicycle. Some had found the wheels, others the frame. The North African had been very helpful, because, having gone to the rag-pickers' address that Michel had given him and having found living quarters there, he had been able to collect a lot of material necessary for the bike. They were all second-hand parts—but good, and in working condition, his friends at the plant guaranteed. The men were all mechanics, and they had put the whole thing together in their spare time on Sundays. And the young apprentice, Pierre, had done the painting—a lovely Chinese-red lacquer, which, he said, would suit André's dark hair.

When at last André got his breath he said, "I don't know how to thank you. Think of your spending not only money, but all your free time on this! It's too much. Now let me give you something down right away toward the purchase of this machine—"

"What?" they all shouted. "Don't be silly. We told you, it's a present. Keep your money for a racing baby some-day. This is just a sports model, but it will do for a while."

"But how—how can I ever thank you?"

"Forget it. It's only natural. You'd do the same. Soli-darity. Only watch out—now we mean business! You get into shape, kid—training, training, as Girard's son should do. And someday we will cry ourselves hoarse, *"Vive Dédé!"*

Vive Dédé! Hurray for Dédé! It gave him gooseflesh. Better not think about it.

The Renouts were overjoyed at his good fortune. Mrs. Renout said, "White Rabbit, you deserve every bit of this bike."

Papa advised, "Make the most of the last good weekends in December and January."

And Miquette added softly, "I'll knit you some mittens."

Finally, Mr. Valeur said, "Splendid! You ride as much as you can while the weather is still dry. There will be plenty of bad weeks when we can study."

This was exactly what André was going to tell his mother. Maman had been pleased that he had a bicycle, because he wanted one so badly, but she said that she still favored a higher education. Well, he would show her that he meant to have both.

He woke up every morning with a song in his heart. His bike! And all the week he looked forward to Sundays. December was cold and dry, and he was grateful for Miquette's mittens. They were a brilliant cobalt-blue, and, besides being comfortable, they looked very pretty against the Chinese-red lacquer of the bike. He was in heaven, and he hoped the weather would stay fair. Every good Sunday was that much added to catch up with Fernand. The exercise in the open did him good too, and he felt himself getting stronger and stronger. He was "building himself up."

The latter part of January turned wet and stormy, and by February it was out of the question for André to get out on his bicycle. So he went back to Mr. Valeur and enjoyed his studies—all the more so because during the week the men had taken to asking him what he had learned. He would explain, and they would discuss it eagerly. They always encouraged him, saying, "Go to it, kid! We don't want an ignorant, uncouth racer. Someday you will do us proud!"

However, as the bad weather on Sundays persisted, he became restless; and one day Mr. Valeur said, "Do you know how to take your bike apart? . . . No? Well, this is the time to learn. A modern bike is made of around seventeen thousand pieces—"

"What?" cried André.

"Yes, just about seventeen thousand pieces. But you don't have to know them all—just so that you are familiar with the essential parts and can take them apart and put them back together quickly."

André tried it one rainy Sunday, using his open-end wrenches and his adjustable wrenches and his screwdriver. And when everything was on the floor he thought he could never put the pieces together again! It took him all afternoon.

By the end of February he could do it in twenty

minutes. Mr. Valeur commented, "Not bad. Perhaps someday you can beat Petit-Breton. He used to do it in seven
minutes."

André gasped.

"Yes, he did. Why don't you keep track of your own
record? As a matter of fact, why don't you get yourself a
notebook and put down everything connected with your
training? That way you can reread it once in a while, see
how you are progressing, and make sure at the same time
that you are not slipping in anything."

XI. Training

ANDRÉ GIRARD.

BICYCLE-RACING TRAINING NOTEBOOK.

LEARNING TO RIDE

1. Sit on saddle comfortably. Saddle should be at proper height—that is, one should be able to touch, with heel, without a shoe, the center of the pedal when it is at its lowest point, so that the leg is straight without being tense.
2. On a sports or racing bicycle, one's back should be about horizontal.
3. No weight on the handlebars. Wrists should be perfectly flexible at all times.
4. Brakes. Do not use on curves. Do not apply suddenly.

PHYSICAL FITNESS
1. Utmost cleanliness. Especially watch teeth and toenails.
2. Early to bed, up early. Sleep with window open.
3. Eat plenty of fresh fruit. No special diet, but nothing in excess.
4. No smoking.

CLOTHING
1. Wool is best. It is better to be too warm than cold.
2. Newspaper should be used for protection only in an emergency, since it prevents the skin from breathing.
3. Shorts. Three layers of material: chamois, wool, cotton. All smooth. There should not be one wrinkle in the seat.
4. Mittens, or pair of gloves with tips of fingers cut off.

PEDALING
Get the feel of the pedals. They should turn evenly, without "bumps" or "holes." Do not push one, then the other. Make them turn smoothly and rhythmically. This continuity and evenness in revolving is called by the racers "to turn circularly." This is done best by "ankle play." In bicycling, ankles are as important as legs. Ankles should never be stiff; they should always be supple enough to bring the down pedal up. This articulated pedaling is quite a trick to learn.

RHYTHM
Choose one rhythm when you start out, and keep it up. Don't go slowly at one time and fast at another.

TAKING CARE OF THE BIKE
When you are one of the top racers on a team this is done by a "domestic." He is not a servant, though, just another racer in a lower category—for the time being.

Bike should be wiped off after each outing, especially after
   rain.
Do not clean chain. Grease and dirt protect it.
When not in use for several days, hang bike.

In March there were a few good weekends and André
could go out again. He increased the distance each time:
forty miles, forty-five miles, fifty miles, and so on. He still
rode with the fixed wheel, as the men at the factory had
advised him to do—"You've got to feel sure and easy before you start using the free wheel."

At last, in April, he tried the free wheel and the gear
shift. In his notebook he jotted down the record at each
run.

		GEAR SHIFT	MILES
April	1	46 × 19	25
	7	47 × 16	30
	14	47 × 17	40
	21	47 × 18	50
	28	47 × 18	55

GEAR SHIFT
   A delicate mechanism. To be used gently.
   Do not overdo it. Continuous changes of gear alter rhythm
      and are a strain on lungs and heart.

As the days lengthened he was able to take short rides
at night after he got home. One evening as he was pedaling in the Bois de Boulogne he caught sight of Fernand
on his racing bike, watch in hand. André groaned. Not

only was Fernand already able to train on a racing bike, but he had reached the point of timing himself.

Soon after, it started to rain and André decided to go to Mr. Valeur's.

"What's the matter?" Mr. Valeur asked as André came in. "You look upset. Had a puncture?"

"No. It's Fernand. I'll never catch up with him." And he told Mr. Valeur about Fernand timing himself. But Mr. Valeur didn't seem to take it seriously at all, and as André kept on scowling he said, "I tell you what. Why don't you take along an alarm clock for yourself?"

"An alarm clock?"

"Of course! Didn't you know? In 1927, when time-trial racing was introduced in the *Tour,* timekeeping watches were very expensive and few people could afford them. So the spectators used to take along their large alarm clocks in order to keep track of the timing."

André couldn't help laughing.

"That's better," said Mr. Valeur. "Keep it up, my boy, keep it up. Doesn't the history of civilization show that it is not necessarily those who have it easy who get some-where?"

Keep it up. Keep it up. How long, how long? André wondered. He was doing his utmost—using every bit of his spare time for training on his sports bike, and continuing to carry on the self-discipline: food, plenty of sleep, no drinking or smoking. And yet he was gnawed inside by the feeling that he was not getting anywhere. Training and working at the same time was too much. The factory exhausted him. Perhaps Maman and the principal had been right. He was not strong enough; he could not make it. And that meant that he could never catch up with Fernand, never wipe out the sting of his name-calling. He had been handicapped at the start by the war and a lack of money.

Jack was better prepared. Jack had a father. He had not suffered from near starvation. And Jack had started training a year ahead of André. Maybe Jack would beat Fernand. Suddenly André raised his head. No! He did not want anybody, not even Jack, to fight his own battle.

He was pulled away from his somber thoughts by shrieks of the children in the street. "André! Give us a ride! Give us a ride! Please!" He did not feel much like it, but he got off his bicycle anyhow, and for fifteen minutes he rode up and down with them and put them on his saddle and pushed them along.

At last he said, "No more. I have to go home."

But the children crowded around him and wouldn't let him go. Then he heard a voice saying, "Eh there! Let André go! He has no more time. Leave him alone. He is going to be a racer. He will be in the *Tour*."

"In the *Tour!*" the children gasped, and let go of him and his bike at once.

Miquette laughed at André's surprised face. "I had to rescue you," she said as she started walking with André. Just then a girl her age came up to her and said, "You don't have to be so stuck-up! There is only one future racer worth anything in La Mouff', and that's Fernand Fausset!"

"What?" cried André and Miquette together.

"Tsk, tsk, tsk," said a peaceful voice. They turned around, and there was Michel, grinning. He put his hand on André's shoulder. "Why be rattled? I've never known you to be afraid of Fernand, even when he was twice your size. Remember?"

That night, in his bed, André counted on his fingers. Miquette came right out and said that I would be in the *Tour*. Michel seemed confident that I will beat Fernand. Mr. Valeur always speaks as if he took it for granted that I will be a racer. The men at the factory do too, and they proved it.

He wondered about Maman, asleep in the other room. Did she believe in him too? Would she ever become reconciled to his being a racer? Yes—if he made it. Well, he would show her! He would make it! He would! Why not? That's what Mr. Williams had said: "Why not?" And Mr. Williams, too, believed in André.

In June his buddies at the factory told him, "It's time for you to ride with other cyclists and start learning about competition. You'd better join the group of young ones in the plant who go out every weekend."

He did, and in no time at all he learned a lot. He wrote in his notebook:

RIDING IN A GROUP

Take short and fast rides. Never amble along.

Plan trip carefully together: where you want to go; what speed you will use; what time you expect to start; what time you expect to arrive at your destination.

Keep a steady, even pace.

PUNCTURES

If a fellow has a puncture, two others in the group wait for him to repair. It is quickly done because we carry spare tubeless tires. Then we all rejoin the group. Catching up is best done in company.

Sunday after Sunday the group took longer and longer rides. But André was so eager that he also made long trips on Saturday afternoons by himself. One Monday when he got to the plant he could hardly keep awake; he was groggy from fatigue.

At lunchtime the men scolded him. "You're crazy! You're going to knock your heart out. You can't ride seventy and eighty miles two days in succession and work all week in the factory. You've got to train gradually. Who do you think you are, Bobet?"

July came around and the *Tour* was on again. Once more the French were defeated. "See, André," said the men, "they need you."

The pleasant sound of their phrase did not last long. That evening Michel came around before starting on his vacation, and right away André sensed that his friend had bad news.

"Is it Fernand?" he asked.

"Yep. You know, of course, that he has already raced in several amateur contests."

"He has? I didn't know!"

"Where have you been? It's the talk of La Mouff'!"

"Guess I'm too busy with my own training," said André darkly.

"Well, the point is that today he won the Paris-Chantilly amateur race."

There was a heavy silence. Then André said slowly, "This means that soon he'll have a good chance of being singled out by a bicycle firm and getting his professional license. And I haven't even got a racing bike."

"Maybe," said Michel slowly, "Jack will be the one to square our account with Fernand."

"What do you mean?"

"Well, we don't hear from Jack, but hasn't he been training for quite a while? And I'll bet he would relish getting even with Fernand. After all, didn't Fernand try to brand him as a thief?"

"He nearly ruined my friendship with Jack too," said André hotly, "and, in addition, I had to stand his scoffing and name-calling all the time I was in school. Jack never had to put up with that. Fernand wouldn't have dared."

"Maybe. But who cares, anyhow? Now you're a tall guy, and—"

"I'm tall, but Fernand is a year older than I am, and because of his money he is way ahead of me."

"Well, Jack doesn't have it easy either, after all."

"Right. Look, Michel, if I'm not going to beat Fernand in the *Tour,* then let it be Jack. But I *am* going to beat him—I am! Mark my words. I don't know how. But I will, as sure as my name is Girard!"

So he said, because Michel's mention of Jack had aroused his spirit. But when he was alone that night he could find no peace. How, how could he make it? Time was running out. It was not only Fernand. Even his good friend Jack was ahead. He did not dare go to the Renouts' to ask; and besides, Miquette was staying away from him too. This was a bad sign. Perhaps already Jack— Sleep, sleep. A racer should sleep well.

Early next Saturday, as he was getting ready to go out with his group, there was a knock at the door. He opened it, and there was Jack! They fell into each other's arms. It had been two years since they had seen each other. They could not get over it, and kept looking each other over.

André cried, "But you shave!"

And Jack retorted, "What do you think? I don't want to look like a caveman, the way *you* do!"

"I?" André protested, and he ran to the mirror. By trying hard, he could see a faint shadow on his chin and jaw.

"What are you trying to do?" Jack went on, jokingly as usual. "Trying to compete with Grandpa Isaac? Bad for the *Tour!* A beard gets in the way, you know."

André smoothed his cheeks with his hand. "It's not that bad! My, Jack, you are a big guy!"

"Well, you're as tall as I am, only you're wiry. The elegant type, as Miquette told me already."

"Oh bosh!" said André, turning away to hide his blushing. "What about some coffee?"

"But you were about to go out."

"Yes, but now that you are here it's different."

"Well, I could go out too—that is, if you want me."

"But you didn't bring your bicycle, did you?"

"Of course I did! What did you expect? Come on, I'll show you." He took André to the window. And there on the curb was a slender racing bicycle. Jack, beaming with pride, went on. "A short while ago I had a break: a Swiss fellow at the works emigrated to the United States. So he let me have his bike for a song. Wasn't I lucky?"

And how! André thought. But he felt no resentment. Since Jack had stepped into the room all the warmth of their old friendship was back.

"Come on with our group," said André. "We are going to Fontainebleau today."

Jack was in fine shape, and André could not help being proud when the others told him so. The group was all elated by the presence of an outsider, and they discussed all sorts of points and tried new technical stunts. André had a lot to write in his notebook afterward.

MEALS

Keep regular hours.

If you eat while riding, choose your favorite food. (Mine: fresh fruit and rice pudding.) Drinks: mineral water or hot tea. Carry a lump of sugar or chocolate in pocket.

WIND

To gain speed without exhausting yourself, trail for a while directly behind another racer's wheel. He breaks the air resistance, and at the same time creates a vacuum that pulls you forward. The cyclist who goes first is called a locomotive.

PUMP STROKES

This is the cyclist's expression for fainting. If you faint, never ride again that same day, not even very slowly. The greatest champions, when it happens to them, never make *one* pedal turn again that day. Take a train to get home and rest. Then you will be fit for the next outing.

Jack left the next day. "I had a perfectly grand time," he said. "I won't write—you know that—especially now that I'm going to enter amateur contests."

They shook hands, and Jack, rolling his eyes, added gaily, "And don't forget to shave!"

The weeks that followed were dark weeks. André tried not to lose heart, and he went on training. But he couldn't help thinking, For what? He was not making any headway.

In December some of the men at the factory teased him. "What's the matter with that saint of yours? Can't the guy see that now you need a racing baby?"

André laughed; at the factory he put up a front. But at home he was quieter than usual—even more so because for some reason that he could not make out Maman seemed more cheerful than she had been for a very long time.

New Year's Day found him brooding more heavily than ever as he sat at the breakfast table with Maman. Suddenly Maman asked, "Why don't you try to trade your sports bike for a racing model?"

He looked up in amazement. Maman suggesting such a thing! What had happened? But, of course, right away, her question showed that she had no idea of all that was involved. So he mumbled none too graciously, "I don't have nearly enough money saved to make up the difference in price."

"Maybe I have," Maman said quietly.

You could have knocked him over with a feather. How could it possibly be? Then he remembered that she had often told him that she had to work overtime. She always made it sound as if she couldn't help it, as if it were because the post office was short of employees. Now he knew better!

Looking at her at that moment, it also dawned upon him suddenly that Maman was still wearing the same "best" dress she had had three years ago. Of course she had it on today only because it was a holiday. The other days she took it off as soon as she came back from work and hung it up carefully, even if it were only for the lunch hour.

He got up quickly and put his arms around her. Maman felt so tiny as he hugged her to him, crying, "Maman, you are the most self-sacrificing human being I know!"

Maman pushed him away, laughing. "Don't give me that self-sacrificing line, young man. Aren't I your mother? It is only natural—what I have done. Of course, I would have preferred that you hadn't wanted to be a racer. But since your heart is set on it, I have to try to help you out. And don't fool yourself; when I make you happy, I please myself too. It's my form of selfishness."

"Hurray for the most unselfish selfishness of Maman!" shouted André.

And that very Saturday they went to buy the racing bike.

It was a beauty. Precision and lightness. Less than twenty pounds. Narrow racing frame. Extra-light rims in duralumin. Front wheel slightly larger than rear wheel. Tubeless tires, toe clips and straps, eight-speed Simplex *Tour de France* gear shift, racing brakes, reversible handlebar post, rack for feeding bottle, special leather racing saddle, pump, and tool kit. And of course no mudguard, no reflector, no light, no horn. A regular racing bicycle. Color: soft buff, practical and smart.

At the factory it was his turn to tease the men. "See, Saint André!"

"Phew! It's only because *we* tipped him off," they retorted with happy faces. "Look, kid. Now it's serious business. You concentrate on amateur contests, every weekend when there is a race. Try to win several races. It may take time. But that's what you've got to do. Then maybe the director of a bicycle firm will notice you, and you will get a contract and your professional license. And then you can quit the factory."

Quit the factory! It didn't seem possible. André tried to figure it out. If I train as much as I can, maybe in the spring I will be ready for amateur races.

He said to Mr. Valeur, "From now on I have to go out, rain or shine. After all, sometimes it pours during the *Tour,* and it can be freezing in the mountains. I have to get used to everything."

"Go ahead, my boy," said Mr. Valeur. "There will always be a few winter Sundays when not even champs could go out. Then we can study."

By March, André felt in such wonderful shape that not even Michel's announcement that Fernand had been picked up by the Lucifer bicycle firm and had got his professional license could dampen his spirits. Meeting Miquette on the street, he asked about Jack.

"We don't know. He doesn't write."

"Maybe he has a contract already. He has been running in amateur races in the south for six months now."

"No, I don't think he got his professional. He would

have told us. But listen, André, for the longest time I have wanted to tell you: I want you both, you and Jack, to win the *Tour*."

Just like a girl! thought André. He tried to explain. "We can't both win—"

"I don't care what you say," Miquette interrupted impatiently, "I want you both to win and defeat Fernand."

"Fernand is going to be the *Tour* hero of La Mouff'!" the girl who had come up to Miquette before called defiantly.

"He's not there yet by a long shot," snapped André, surprised at his own self-assurance.

Yet he did not feel so peppy throughout the spring, when the papers began to talk more and more about Fausset: "A newcomer in professional racing," "a promising youngster," "a powerful engine."

At last, in May, André was accepted by an amateur club. His first race was a complete flop. He had worked himself up to such a pitch that once he was on his bicycle his sight was completely blurred and he had to go slowly for many miles. He was left behind by all the others, and when at last he had quieted down and could see clearly again, it was too late to catch up, though he gave all he had.

At the factory the men were angry for the first time, and they bawled him out roughly. "Don't look for any sympathy around here! Acting like a girl, that's what you did! If you can't be a man, say so and forget about bicycle-racing!"

Their lashing cut him to the quick, and somehow it knocked all the nonsense out of him. In the next race he was calm and self-composed, and right away he began showing his mettle: a powerful pedal stroke in climbing and a dogged resistance to fatigue. Coming home that Saturday night, he knew in his bones that bicycle-racing was work, very hard work, but that he could tackle it.

He found La Mouff' in a dither. Everybody seemed to be reading the *Parisien Libéré*. He caught a glimpse of the headline—FAUSSET: A NEW STAR RISING ON THE TOUR HORIZON.

Fernand was winning professional races, and already there was talk of his being lined up for the *Tour* in the near future.

André was moody all week and waited eagerly for the Paris-Chartres amateur race.

He came in second in this race. As he stepped off his bicycle, covered with the dust of the flat wheat country, in front of the old Chartres Cathedral, a burly-looking man came up to him and asked, "What's your name?"

"Girard."

"Girard? Any relation to the great Girard who—"

"He was my father."

"You don't say! How old are you?"

"Sixteen."

"How long have you been racing?"

"Two years."

"All the time?"

"No, I work all day in a plant."

"Ah. Do you like racing in amateur contests?"

"It's okay, for the time being."

"What do you mean?"

"I want to race professionally—in the *Tour*."

The man slapped him on the shoulder. "Keep it up, keep it up. Plenty of sleep, a lot of fruit, no smoking, no drinking, eh?" And swiftly he disappeared in the crowd.

"Who is he?" André asked the other cyclists. "A journalist?"

"Don't you know him? He is the director of the La Perle bicycle firm."

"Is that so?" André tried to look casual, but his heart was beating fast. La Perle. That was the firm that had sponsored his father before the accident.

All that week he rushed home from work, expecting a letter from La Perle to have been forwarded to him by the club. But nothing came.

During the whole summer he raced in all the amateur contests he could. And in some of them, especially those in the mountains, he distinguished himself. But he never came in first. At the finish of each race he scanned the crowd eagerly, hoping to see the face of the man from La Perle again. But he never did.

October came around again, and Michel got back from his vacation at Grandpa Isaac's. He announced, "I am going to be a journalist."

"Just like the North African said!" André exclaimed.

"Yes. I'm starting as a cub reporter."

"You're a professional before I am," André remarked with a touch of melancholy.

"Right. But I have little chance of making a spectacular career, as you have. As a matter of fact, I have none at all. Did you ever hear of millions of people acclaiming a journalist? Can you see all the boys making a pinup of my photo as you did of Bobet's? Can you imagine all the girls throwing kisses at my mug?"

André could not help laughing.

"How are you doing?" asked Michel. "Still running amateur? When is the next race?"

"In two weeks. Paris-Tours."

He never raced so well as he did in this contest, so steadily and so easily. He flew along like an arrow, and though he put all his energy into it, he raced without any strain. It was such a beautiful day! The air was saturated with the smell of the late ripe grapes, and along the hills the vineyards were turning gold.

He entered Tours way ahead of the others. He got off his bicycle with poise and elegance, thinking of nothing except that it had been a marvelous ride.

"Hello there, Girard."

André turned around—and looked right into the smiling face of the man from La Perle. They shook hands.

"I've watched you all summer long."

"You have! But I never saw you!"

"I didn't want you to. But I didn't miss one of your races. The only thing I didn't like was your pushing so hard. But now your anxiety is gone. So we can start from there. How would you like to come with us? Oh, I forgot to introduce myself. I am with La Perle, and I did not want to tell you before, but I knew your father. A wonderful guy, in every way." The man paused, and André nodded. Then the man went on briskly, "When you are with us I can ask the *Fédération Française du Cyclisme* for your professional license. Of course, you have to qualify. It means rigorous training, and learning teamwork, and getting ready all the while for more and more difficult contests."

André reddened. "The *Tour?*" he asked.

"Don't know. Maybe yes, maybe no. We'll see. La Perle takes charge. And no fooling. Come on, let's have a glass of Périer and talk it over. When can you quit the factory?"

André went back to Paris in a daze. On the table there was a letter from Jack. He tore it open.

Dear André,

Big news! I have my professional license. The Peugeot firm took me on after I won Bordeaux-Bayonne, amateur. What about you?

Always,
Jack

"Always, Jack." That was it. André was both happy and irked. Well, he couldn't worry right now. He asked, "Maman, aren't you glad that I was chosen?"

"Yes, since this is what you want. But bicycle-racing is so dangerous." She sighed. "Your father was with La Perle when—"

He stroked her hair tenderly. "There, there, Maman, this time it will be all right."

He went over to the Renouts'.

"I got a letter from Jack."

"So did we," said Mrs. Renout cautiously.

"It's wonderful that he got his professional license!"

"Ah," said Mr. Renout, looking at his wife, "he told you about it too. Now, my boy, don't you get discouraged—"

"I am quitting the factory. La Perle has taken me over."

"Hurray!" shouted Miquette. "Didn't I tell you? Both of you!"

"But—" protested André, laughing.

"White Rabbit," said Mrs. Renout, "this is a good day. You and our Jack. When you came in we sort of didn't know how to act because we didn't want to hurt you. But now we can just raise Cain!"

"With a glass of milk for me, please!" André shouted gaily.

At the factory the news exploded like a bombshell. Everyone came to congratulate him, even workers he didn't know at all. One of them had made the grade, had become "professional." That was something!

But at lunchtime, when he met with the little group that had given him his start, he burst out, "I hate to quit the plant." And he said it from the bottom of his heart.

They said, "We hate to see you go too. But don't you believe for a minute that we're not going to keep tabs on you any more! We will." And they scolded him playfully, "Better keep straight, and get there—to the top, where you belong. We'll be watching you!"

He came home to find Michel pacing up and down in front of his house.

"Congratulations!"

"How did—"

"And some for Jack too."

"I'll be darned. How do you know all this?"

"My profession. Keeping my eyes peeled, as usual. But, really, *Sambre et Meuse!* You and Jack are climbing so fast that nobody is going to be able to keep up with you —except, of course, your poor journalist friend. When are you leaving the factory?"

"In two weeks. After that, there'll be nothing to do but train—and get ready for the Big Loop!"

XII. The Big Loop

Paris, April 15

Mr. and Mrs. Charles Williams
Yellow Springs, Ohio

Dear Mr. and Mrs. Williams,

Do you still remember the French boy you met when you were sitting at a terrace café in Paris? I am the French boy, and you told me that when I raced in the *Tour de France,* the Big Loop, I should let you know.

Well, this is it. I have been chosen, though I am still in my teens. I will run this year with the French team, the Tricolores.

There are teams and runners from all over: Switzerland, Italy, Belgium, England, Holland, Spain, Australia, Sweden, Indochina, Israel, Senegal, and Morocco. But we have no Reds. It's a pity. Perhaps *you* can do something about it in the years to come.

If it is possible for you to come I will be very happy. The

175

Tour starts in Nancy on July 7 and ends in Paris on July 28.

My mother wishes to be remembered to you. Hoping to see you soon—why not?—I beg you to accept, dear Mr. and Mrs. Williams, the expression of my best and respectful feelings.

André Girard

Papers! Papers! This balmy summer evening people snatched the newspapers with the big headlines: LAST-MINUTE EMERGENCY IN THE TRICOLORES. LEBLANC FALLS SICK. YOUNG RENOUT TAKES HIS PLACE.

"Renout? Jack Renout on the Tricolore team? But he's a newcomer, and the Tricolores already have a youngster this year, André Girard. That's bad for the team."

"Maybe not. They were getting a bit seedy. They need young blood."

"Renout must be happy. He lost out with the Tricolores last April. They were looking for a nervous, wiry, inflammable, and determined type, and they chose Girard. He's still in his teens."

"It's not so bad, then, for them to have Renout too. He's a sort of young giant, built like Hercules. That will give the team a nice balance."

"Yes, especially since on the Southwest team they have that new power engine, Fernand Fausset."

"How is Renout going to get to Nancy in time to start with the others?"

"He has taken a plane. He is probably already in Nancy by this time."

So people were talking, all over France. Meanwhile Jack, having arrived in Nancy and received all the latest instructions from the manager of the team, burst into André's room.

"I can't believe it!" he bellowed. "Just can't! What a break! There I was, eating my heart out because they had not taken me! Of course, last April I could see their point of view and I was awfully happy that you were the one. But I wanted to be in it too, so badly. And now here we are. Our first *Tour!* And together, on the same team!"

"Maybe that's not so good," André commented gravely.

"Why not?"

"Well, both of us can't win, after all, can we?"

" 'Course not. But why worry? It's teamwork, isn't it? Solidarity."

André was silent. Jack came up to him eagerly. "What's the matter?"

"Fernand is racing."

"Don't I know it! And don't I love it! He's not racing with the Tricolores, though; they got his number all right, eh? The Southwest team doesn't know what kind of double-crosser they're getting."

"They're also getting a top-notch racer. He has already made history, as you know. His racing record is far better than mine, anyhow."

"No better than mine, no better than mine! Don't worry, André, I can beat Fernand!"

"And win the *Tour?*" queried André in a colorless voice.

They stood facing each other, and suddenly there were

tension and defiance between them. This had not happened since way back, in their boyhood, at the time of the Bobet-picture incident. An ugly choking mounted in their throats as they measured each other. Their long friendship was at stake, ready to topple over in the next second. Panic gripped them both as they eyed each other. Then the door opened a crack and a head peered in.

"Michel!" they both exclaimed. "What are you doing here?"

"What do you think—that you are both going to race in the *Tour* without me?"

"But Michel—" Jack began.

"I know! I bet I know!" cried André. "He's in a reporters' car. He's covering the *Tour* for his paper!"

Michel winked.

"Aren't you smart!" Jack commented. "How did you do it?"

"Kept my eyes peeled, as usual. So you too are in. Grand, since at this stage of the game it isn't a question of one of you winning the *Tour*."

"What do you mean?" asked André.

"Well, after all, two youngsters like you—it's quite an achievement just to be picked for the Tricolores and the *Tour*. Nobody expects you to win. You probably won't even get close to the winner's record. But you can do grand work for the team. Well, so long. Better turn in early tonight. I'll be seeing you! *Sambre et Meuse! Sambre et Meuse!*"

Michel was gone. André and Jack looked at each other

and burst out laughing. Jack rolled his eyes merrily and roared, "Just look at us! Here we were glaring at each other and almost ready to bite each other! Michel is right. As if the *Tour* was going to be a competition between us two greenhorns!"

"We're just nuts!" said André convincingly as they shook hands warmly.

In his room, Michel reread the carbon copy of the article he had written for his newspaper. It was to appear the next morning as an introduction to his daily reporting of the *Tour.*

Once again the heart of France goes out to those giants of the road who will speed by, through their own muscular efforts, on slight, slender contraptions weighing less than twenty pounds. Every year, everywhere, men and boys, followed by entire families, pour out of houses, apartments, farms, and spill over into streets and roads. They walk miles; they ride bicycles or motorcycles; they drive in old jalopies or horse-drawn farm wagons or delivery trucks or small private cars. They come in trains and buses: picnicking, camping out, lining beaches and climbing mountains. They wait for hours under the scorching sun or shiver on a cold summit. All young France is on tiptoe, to see for a brief instant more than a hundred athletes tearing by on their fragile machines.

Now, for those who have to stay at home, there is the possibility of participation through television. This year not only will arrivals and departures be televised, but running alongside the racers will be two cameramen riding motorcycles and taking pictures right along.

As usual, in this paper as in other newspapers, all political events will take second place. The *Tour* comes first. It does on the radio too. All France pauses in her year's work and lets herself be carried away by the big excitement. And why not? The *Tour de France* is the biggest single democratic annual sports event in the whole world. The Big Loop is unique. All in all, the *Tour* mobilizes a small army: 1500 people under way, 100 motorcycles, 250 cars. In addition, it employs about 12,000 extra people at each stop. And it attracts the active interest of around 30 million people in the whole nation. All this for one winner out of the 115 champions who run in this fantastic race!

It should not be forgotten that the *Tour* is also largely responsible for the big development in France of the bicycle industry, which has a yearly sale of around 1,500,000 bicycles. It brings commercial prosperity all along its way. Towns and cities vie for the privilege of having the racers go through, pause for refreshments, or make an overnight stop. One of the reasons the itinerary is changed every year is in order to give different places a chance. The *Tour,* indeed, is a great benefactor in many ways: wherever the *Tour* goes there is not only money spent, there is gaiety, festivity, a lifting of the spirit, and a warming up of the heart. It is also a sign that there is no war and no invasion on French soil. As my beloved teacher in public school used to say, "The *Tour* is the child of the people and peace."

So let us rejoice that it is with us once more. And let us give a big hand all along the way to the "Centaurs of the Road." The readers of this newspaper will find in this column an accurate, objective, first-hand report of what takes place every day of the *Tour*.

Michel Mayer

The next morning the sky hung low and the air was stifling over Nancy, the old capital of the Dukes of Lorraine, in the eastern part of France. In spite of the ominous clouds, thousands of people lined Stanislas Square and the streets, as the publicity parade of the *Tour* got under way. As usual, it started an hour and a half before the racers, after orders had been telephoned to clear and detour all traffic ahead on the road.

Children shouted with delight as the floats went by: the giant ink bottle; the transparent plastic car of Sofil wool; the rolling, enormous cask of the French wine-growers, adorned with grapevines; the ten-foot tube of cold cream; the mammoth fountain pen; the hilarious and famous cow, La Vache-qui-rit (the Laughing Cow); the proud papier-mâché lion of Lion Noir shoe polish; the eighteen-foot alarm clock; the huge Périer water bottle; Coca-Cola company cars; the entertainment car—floor show and movies—and many other cars and floats.

Everything is free to the public on the *Tour*. Nothing can be sold. Everything is given away for publicity at each stop, and the crowd fights good-naturedly to get samples, see the movies and the show, and taste the drinks.

Following the commercial parade came the car of the General Commercial Commissioner. Then came some of the press cars, full of the reporters who cover what happens on the road ahead of the racers.

Then came a car with a large sign: DIRECTOR OF THE RACE, FORWARD. That title means that the director is to control the cars of the publicity caravan to see that they keep far enough ahead so that they do not act as "locomotives" for the first racers, thus giving them an unfair advantage.

After that came a motorcyclist who seemed to do nothing but ride back and forth between the head of the caravan and the racers. He does that straight through the *Tour,* making sure that everyone keeps at the proper distance and that there is no traffic jam. He is called a *slater* because he carries a slate on which he writes his instructions in big letters.

As everything was going on smoothly ahead, the *slater* came back to report to the general director at Stanislas Square. The racers were gathered within the elegant, gilded, iron gates and railing of the famous square, which dates back to the eighteenth century and the Polish king Stanislas Leszcinski, whose daughter married the King of France, Louis XV. It was too bad that there was no sun, but even so it was a pretty sight—all around the square the eighteenth-century mansions, the golden gates; and in the middle the crowd of racers wearing pullovers of the different colors of their nations' flags. Crisscrossed around their backs and shoulders were tubeless tires for emergency repairs.

André and Jack were among the Tricolores—blue, white, and red. Fernand wore the colors of the Southwest team. All the racers faced the west gate, across which a tricolor ribbon was stretched. Standing by were officials, watches in hand, and the Mayor of Nancy, holding a pair of scissors.

Nine o'clock. The mayor cut the ribbon. The racers were off. The crowd cheered madly. Twenty-one days to

go, through rain and shine, plains and mountains, country and cities. Three thousand miles to cover within a natural stadium of three hundred and fifty thousand square miles; a human corridor of fifteen million spectators and countless television onlookers.

As the racers got under way, thunder rolled and lightning flashed. Sky sluices opened wide, and the rain poured down in torrents. But it could not scare the spectators. Soaking wet, they shouted encouragement to the racers, who hopped and shook over the slippery cobblestones.

Behind the racers came the car of the general director, and behind him, on the right side of the road, the cars of the technical directors of the teams and the mechanics' trucks and jeeps. On the left side were more press cars. Michel was in one of them, with other reporters; they were all bundled up in raincoats, their heads covered with oilskin hats. He was weathering the storm the best he could, since they had not had time to put the top up.

In the crowd, a little boy pointed at them. "Look, Daddy! Look at the fishermen!" Laughter shook the drenched pressmen, and Michel waved gaily to the boy and shouted, "You bet! Only this car is no boat! It's a *bathtub!*"

The road was empty for a while. Then came the police, on motorcycles; then a car labeled DIRECTOR OF THE RACE, REAR; then the *slater,* for the rear-liaison traffic information; then the sweeper truck; and finally the Red Cross ambulance.

Blinded by rain, André and Jack plodded along, between hop fields, pastures, and birch-covered hills, on the road to Reims, the first stage of the race.

The town of Commercy had received permission to give the racers some of its delicious and famous cookies, *madeleines.* Jack and André caught some, which were thrown to them by boys standing on the curb.

Then the racers crossed the famed River Meuse, which had just watered Domremy and the meadows where Joan of Arc had tended her sheep as a little girl. From then on the river wound through a busy region where both shores were thick with factories. People call this stretch of the Meuse the "sixty-mile industrial street." After this the cyclists sped through the part of the country where each village is a historic spot recalling wars, invasions, sieges, occupations, treaties—ever since Roman times.

At last, in the Champagne country, the sun began to shine on the vineyards. Nobody had taken the lead so far. But then the Swiss team worked its way through, and finally Piaget shot ahead.

"Burns me up!" muttered Jack.

"Go ahead, kid," said the leader of the Tricolores, "if it will make you happy. You can't catch up with Piaget, but you can have some fun."

Jack darted forward, and the Tricolores had a surprise coming to them. Not only did Jack have fun, but he made quite a hit—he, so young, chasing topnotch veteran Piaget. That was a feather in the cap of the Tricolores, even if Jack didn't catch up with Piaget. As André said later, "Why, it gave us all a boost!"

The second day they rode through the big Ardennes Forest, which is still so wild in parts that boars and wolves have elected it as their last hideout in France.

As they entered Lille, the capital of French Flanders and a busy textile city, the radio announced, "The Hollander Van Velt wins this stretch. Fausset of the Southwest team close behind. Piaget still first in the general score."

Both Jack and André had wanted to race after Fernand, but the Tricolores had been against it on the ground that it was best to save their strength for later. Both boys had found it very hard to comply. But this was teamwork, and the watchword was solidarity.

The third day saw them in a stretch called the "Northern Hell" because the road was a horror of broken-up

pavement and the air full of falling cinders. In addition, rain poured again. André gritted his teeth. The Tricolores did not intend to try anything spectacular, and they let Schroeder and the Belgian team take the lead. But suddenly, parting the rain curtain, a lone racer whizzed by. Fernand! A quick nod from the team, and in a split second Jack was off after him.

Spectators watched with awe the fierce struggle between Fernand and Jack, both dripping wet, covered with mud and cinders, and wobbling over the sharp, slippery stones betwen the endless rows of coal miners' identical houses as they tried to outdistance each other. That night Michel telephoned his paper:

"Belgian Shroeder wins the Lille-Dieppe stretch. Renout of the Tricolores makes a second getaway, trying to beat Fausset of the Southwest team. It's a tie.

"Piaget retains first place in the general score. The Northern Hell takes its toll; two racers arrive after the red lantern has been set up and therefore have to abandon the *Tour*."

André did not see Jack that night. All the racers were very tired and retired to their own bedrooms as soon as they came in. But André could not help wishing the Tricolores had sent him chasing after Fernand. They told him they wanted him to give his best in the mountains, where he would be most useful. But he was sure he could do both, if only they let him have his chance.

On the fourth day they rode through green and fertile Normandy; they flew over the bridge across the Seine at Rouen, the city with the hundred church spires. Then they were in the apple-orchard country, enclosed by those hedgerows which had made the advance of the American army so difficult in 1944.

No one distinguished himself among the Tricolores, who seemed to have taken the attitude that they were not in shape to score much in this *Tour,* since they were short of the seasoned racers who had made them famous in the past. André and Jack held their own as they had been asked to do. But when the Australian Travers entered the old city of Caen first, André could hardly contain himself, and the director of the team said, "All right, all right! Chafing at the bit, eh? Well then, we will let you try to make your own birthplace tomorrow, Nantes."

Two days later the papers' headlines read: YOUNG GIRARD ENTERS NANTES FIRST. PIAGET RETAINS FIRST PLACE IN THE GENERAL SCORE.

And Michel wrote:

The police had a hard time protecting Girard from the proud enthusiasm of his Breton compatriots. Some of them remembered Girard's father, the phenomenal prewar racer whose bitter bad luck prevented him from running the *Tour.*

As dirty as he was, young Girard was not only kissed on both cheeks by the welcoming committee, but he disappeared under a swarming mob of women from whom he was finally rescued by the police.

When we saw him, at his hotel, he was just emerging from a bathtub—according to regulations, only one-third full, in order to avoid weakening the body's resistance—and was being massaged and greased on a special sheet spread on the table provided by the *Tour* organization.

"Sit down in that armchair," he said to me. "*You* can do it. As far as *I* am concerned, armchairs are off bounds for the duration." Girard was alluding to a section of the rules racers have to sign before they are allowed to compete in the *Tour,* which forbids them to sit on any hotel furniture for fear of ruining it.

We found Girard in the best of spirits. We congratulated him on his spectacular early getaway after Caen, and on his unheard-of speeding up two miles before the sprint instead of the usual 1500 feet. By so doing, he not only arrived first in his home town, but he showed that a new technique could be used in the sprint; and, in addition, he enlarged on his youthful reputation, which has been based mainly on the fact that he is a strong climber.

We went to have a word with Fausset, mentioning that not only Renout but also Girard was racing very close to him. Fausset said he was not worried by Girard's stunt, which, after all, is customary—many racers win the stretch in their own home towns. He said that, as a matter of fact, he was pleased that Girard and Renout were after him; that "it was bound to work to his advantage sooner or later." He left us with this cryptic statement.

We had a word with Piaget, who still retains first place in the general score. He had nothing but praise for his young opponents. But he remains confident in a quiet way.

André was happy at having entered Nantes first. But he didn't make too much of his victory. As Fernand had pointed out, to get to one's own town is a stimulant that is felt by many racers who do not score anywhere else. He knew that at this stage of the game nothing could be said. His one minute and a half ahead of Fernand, his two minutes ahead of Jack, did not mean much. Piaget

retained first place in the general score, and the *Tour* had just begun. He went to bed right after his massage, as they were to leave very early the next day.

They got up before dawn, in the dark, shivering and groggy with sleep. As of old, when the race had gone on at night, torches were used to light the preparations. These torches shooting sparks in the night, together with the colored Bengal lights, created a weird, fantastic, and beautiful effect. In spite of the early hour, people crowded the streets, many of them having just thrown coats over their night clothes.

The racers bumped over the cobblestones of the old

harbor and made their way out of the city where in the sixteenth century the French king, Henry IV, had signed the famous Edict of Nantes guaranteeing freedom of conscience to Protestants. Then they went through the celebrated Muscadet vineyards, all enshrouded with fog, and across the River Loire; and then they were on the road to the next stop, Bordeaux, through the eerie Bocage region netted with small pools and narrow meadows encircled by oaks, birches, and elms.

Everybody was looking forward to the second breakfast, which at La-Roche-sur-Yon was to be thrown in bags to the racers as they sped by. But long before they came to the town, Fernand, who was very hungry, sneaked around and got food from the driver of a car—which is strictly forbidden. He thought he could get away with it, but the patrol was right on the job.

When Fernand got to Bordeaux he was penalized one minute. He said suavely to the patrol man, "Haw, haw, that's real quaint! But in this Atomic Age I got no time to lose, see?"

"Sorry," said the man curtly, "it's the rule."

"I don't know any rules a little money can't fix," Fernand said pointedly.

"Trying to bribe, eh? Hankering after disqualification, by any chance?" the man stormed.

"Keep your shirt on," snapped Fernand. "I just meant to ask whether my penalization could be in money instead of time."

"The answer is no. Just congratulate yourself that it's not three minutes instead of one."

Bordeaux was the first rest town: twenty-four hours to sleep, bathe, get massages, walk, and loaf. It was the first opportunity for André, Jack, and Michel to get together, which they did around a cup of linden tea (no coffee for racers at night).

Michel was all aglow. "The way you two carry on! Your first *Tour!* You are wonders!"

Jack laughed. "Especially since Kaarti, the Senegalese, won this stretch!"

"And Piaget is still ahead in the general score," went on André thoughtfully.

"What do you expect?" cried Michel. "You don't think that youngsters like you are going to beat the old-timers, do you?"

"Just so Fernand doesn't beat me," said André and

Jack at the same time. And then, instead of laughing at having talked together and said the same thing, there was an embarrassed silence.

Michel looked at them attentively, and then he said evenly, "Take it easy, you two. You, Jack, were spectacular enough in being the first of the Tricolores to make a getaway, and you, André, in winning at Nantes. What more do you want? There are many seasoned champs in this race, some who have won the *Tour* before. You both have made a splendid show so far. For the rest, leave it to the mountains to sort out the racers. They always do."

They nodded, relaxed and smiling. Good old Michel!

Lourdes! What a racket! As the racers arrived, Piaget ahead, thousands of spectators lined the streets, shouting and yelling, and in their midst were thousands of pilgrims to the Grotto. But at Lourdes sick people have the right of way, so the athletes of the road going to their hotels moved about carefully as they brushed past invalids pushed in chairs or carried on stretchers. The din was enormous as the microphones spilled out popular tunes and pious hymns. Bernadette and the *Tour de France!*

Michel hurried to telephone his report to his Paris newspaper. He had some important points to make.

After the mud and the cinders and the sharp stones of the Northern Hell, here is the furnace trial of the Bordeaux-Lourdes stretch.

Today all the racers suffered bitterly from the heat. Spectators are no longer allowed to throw pails of cold water on the cyclists, since it proved dangerous, so members of the teams

cooled one another by pouring bottles of mineral water on the backs of each other's necks. And along the way all the racers kept catching bottles thrown to them and drinking as they went.

It seems that the Tricolores got more than they bargained for when they took in the two youngsters, Girard and Renout. Now the team cannot make up its mind which one to support.

Up to date Girard is running two minutes ahead of Renout. But, on the other hand, he is only one minute and a half ahead of Fausset of the Southwest team, who made up his one-minute penalty.

The mountains as usual will probably do the selecting; though, of course, none of these young men can reasonably expect to win the *Tour*.

Piaget, who won so brilliantly last year, is still in the best form and way ahead in the general score. The Swiss team appears to have the best chance of all so far.

Meanwhile André let himself relax in the capable hands of his masseur. His eyes were sore and his lips and

gums were scorched and cut. He would have to bathe his
eyes with camomile and rub his gums and lips with glyc-
erine and lemon.

The masseur complimented him on his toenails being
in such fine shape. He said, "Some guys have an awful
time. They haven't taken good care of them when they
should have, and in the *Tour* the nails fall off. A torture!"

In his own room, Jack submitted to the doctor's rou-
tine checkup of his heart. The doctor inquired, "What's
on your mind? You are worried. Out with it."

"Well, Doctor, I'll tell you. It's like this: I want to beat
Fausset. An old account to settle, see? But if I do, it may
mean that I beat my best friend too."

"You forget, my young friend, that you probably will
never have a chance of doing either. Just by itself, without
competing, the mountains are a hard enough test for be-
ginners in the *Tour*."

"And suppose I do have a chance to get ahead of
everybody?"

"If you do," exclaimed Michel, who had just come in,
"if you do, I know you'll do the right thing on the spur of
the moment, and that will be what is best for your team
in the *Tour*. Right?"

"Right. Solidarity!" approved Jack, obviously relieved.

Not only were the men getting a thorough overhauling
before tackling the mountain stretch, but the bicycles
were too. Late through the night the mechanics checked
and rechecked.

When the racers woke up, the air was chilly. André went to the window and looked at the high blue chain of the Pyrenees with their white summits. Today was one of the biggest days of the *Tour*: the climbing of the passes of Aubisque, Tourmalet, Aspin, and Peyresourde—the Death Circle, as it is called.

He put on an extra sweater of very lightweight wool, took his mittens—new ones, especially knitted for the *Tour* by Miquette—and went downstairs. He wanted to look his bike over. He asked his helper to fill the feeding bottle with hot tea and get him a few lumps of sugar, to carry in his pocket. Then he heard Jack's voice calling gaily, "Come on to breakfast! Quick! News!"

At the Tricolores' table, the director held up a yellow piece of paper. He said, "It's from Bobet. This is what he says. 'An old war horse wishes the Tricolores luck. Louison Bobet.' "

Bobet! André and Jack looked at each other. Bobet! Old Valeur's class. The picture. The theft. The quarrel. The fight for friendship's sake. The plan to secure justice. The detective work. The vindication. So long ago! And yet it all came back so vividly that it seemed as if it had taken place only yesterday.

"That wire," said the director, "is a good omen for the Tricolores. Go to it, boys. Let's see how we're going to attack. We have held Girard in reserve, so to speak, just for this day. And maybe it would be a good idea to give Renout a free hand too. The two young ones could pace each other."

Some of the older Tricolores started to argue that neither André nor Jack could possibly hold his own in the mountains against the champs of the other teams, and that it would be best for a seasoned climber among the Tricolores to take the lead. But other men pointed out that André's reputation had been made in climbing and that he and Jack had fire in their young blood and could do a lot for the Tricolores—in the first pass, anyway. Meanwhile the older racers could save their strength and take over in the next pass; they could then try to out-distance whoever was ahead from the other teams.

This plan finally rallied everyone. The Tricolores felt that although Piaget was practically unbeatable, they could not afford to let anybody else get ahead. They were especially wary of the Spanish team and of the Southwest team, with that power engine, Fausset.

The signal was given and the racers pedaled away between rows of cheering spectators. Piaget got quite an ovation. He smiled gently and easily. After all, what lay ahead was familiar ground to a Swiss: mountains.

Up, up. Fog clings to the racers. It gets colder and colder. Without any apparent effort, Piaget takes the lead and disappears. At the first pass, Aubisque, five thousand feet high, the early spectators recognize the white Swiss cross through the mist, and, close behind, the Spanish colors of the racer Luco. Four minutes later they see a Tricolore, Girard; two minutes behind him a Southwest racer, Fausset; one minute later comes another

Tricolore, Renout. Seeing that their two youngsters are making good, the Tricolores let them shoot ahead.

Up, up, up. The spectators who line the roads are bundled up in wool sweaters, coats, blankets. Some have kindled fires to warm themselves.

Near the summit of the Tourmalet pass at sixty-five thousand feet there are snow flurries. Piaget leads like a well-greased engine. But Luco is close behind; he raises himself on his pedals, and, going up "like a dancer," he manages to pass Piaget. Quick as a flash Piaget sprints for the summit of the pass ahead of Luco, and sprints again over the top and disappears downhill at breakneck speed.

Three minutes later André labors up the pass. He goes up steadily and rhythmically, careful not to exceed his own limits for fear of being suffocated. He has gained one minute on Piaget, but he knows that Fernand is not far behind.

It is very cold. In spite of the physical effort André is frozen. He thinks that some hot tea from his bottle might help. Without stopping or slowing down he tries to drink. The tea is frozen.

He feels the cold more and more. His fingers, which the mittens leave bare, are completely numb around the handlebars. Up, up. He is almost there. Suddenly there is a splitting sound, and André is hurled through the air. He hits the road and rolls over at the feet of the terrified spectators. He is up at once and running toward his bicycle. The front fork has split. André looks down the road

behind him for the mechanics' jeep and the truck of new bicycles that follows the racers in case of damage to a bicycle—which can happen to the best of them, because of the strain.

No cars in sight. Seconds go by. One minute lost . . . one minute and a half.

The crowd tries to comfort André. "You're lucky not to be hurt." He doesn't hear them.

Two minutes lost. And Fernand emerges, snarls triumphantly, and disappears over the top.

André looks around wildly. If only one of the spectators had a bike, any bike! He would borrow it. But at this height they have all come in buses and cars.

Two minutes and a half. André hears shouts from the crowd below. It *has* to be the truck! No. A racer. Through the fog he climbs furiously. There he is. Jack! He shoots

by and disappears over the top. Bitterness fills André's heart.

Somebody is running toward André, back from the top of the pass. Jack! He jumps off his bike, thrusts it into André's hands. No time for a word, a glance, a thought. André is on, and gone.

Jack stands on the side of the road, empty-handed. He is extraordinarily quiet. Only he feels queer, as if he were all inflated inside and had become light and huge, a sort of blown-up giant towering above the whole landscape. He mutters, "I'm goofy. Must be the altitude." People cheer him madly. He looks at them dully. "What's the matter with them? Why such a fuss? I only want to know what that lousy truck is doing. Ah, here it comes at last!"

Five minutes lost, and with it the chance of beating Fernand.

Meanwhile André is flying down into "the jaws of death." The spectators shudder. They do not dare even to shout. They just clap rhythmically.

Ahead of André there is a speck. Fernand! André gives it all he has. I've got to! I've got to! For *both* our sakes, Jack's and mine. There is blood in his eyes; his throat is parched; his lips are cut; his head pounds painfully. Never mind, never mind. Just let me pass that skunk. Faster, faster. There is a clamor around him. He has left Fernand behind, and he pushes madly ahead in pursuit of Luco and Piaget.

Where are they? How far ahead? Who is first? André shoots ahead like an arrow, hardly touching the ground.

Behind him he hears the danger signal of the Red Cross ambulance. What is it? Why? He is all right. Nothing wrong with him except the trickle of foam from his lips. Down, down, faster, faster, around that curve. There is blood on the road. At forty miles an hour André whizzes by a man stretched on the grass, eyes closed. People are sponging blood from him. Piaget!

In Luchon that night, Jack, Michel, and André gathered in André's room. On the bed lay the carbon copy of what was going to make headlines in Michel's paper.

PYRENEES CRUEL TO PIAGET. MUCH-LOVED CHAMP BADLY HURT, HAS TO ABANDON TOUR. LUCO OF SPANISH TEAM WINS THE STRETCH, THE YOUNGSTER GIRARD DIRECTLY BEHIND.

The remarkable performance which places young Girard among the possible winners of the *Tour* could not have taken place without what we unhesitatingly call the heroic self-sacrificing gesture of Jack Renout, which enabled Girard, despite his lost time, to outdistance powerful Fausset. The latter finds himself in danger now of losing his advantageous place in the general score. It all happened at the Tourmalet, when . . .

"Why did you do it, Jack? Why did you do it?" André kept repeating.

Jack shrugged his shoulders, laughing. "I don't know. Anyhow, you were ahead of me in the general score, don't forget. The accident wasn't your fault, or the delay. The truck should have been there. I was on your team and the first one to see the mishap. So, solidarity."

"You soft-headed goons!" shrieked a voice, as the door flung open and Fernand's angry face appeared. He shook his fists at the group and ran away. The three friends howled merrily.

Then André said, "Solidarity? Maybe. But you had a

perfect right not to do it. You jeopardized your chances completely. In fact, if I had had my wits about me, I—"

"Oh, for Pete's sake, forget it!" Jack exclaimed. "I don't know why I did it; honest I don't. Something in me, going way back—maybe to old Valeur's class. I can't tell. But when I saw you on that pass I just had to turn around and trot back to you. That's all."

"That's all," echoed Michel. "It goes to prove that sometimes it is not the mountains that pick out the winner, it is the heart."

"Now you're talking, young man," approved the doctor, who had just come in with his stethoscope.

The days that followed showed once more how unpredictable and different the *Tour* is every time. That year it came to be referred to as the "*Tour* of the Nations." Every day a racer from the team of another nation won the stretch: the Indochinese racer Baominh entered the walled city of Carcassonne; the Swedish racer Nostrom, Montpellier; the English racer Little, Avignon. Covered with the white-flour dust of the Camargue Desert, the Israeli racer Sukenik entered Aix-en-Provence. The Aix-Gap stretch, in the midst of olive orchards, was covered first by the Algerian racer Ben Ahmed. The Italian Modiano scored at Briançon.

All the while André and Fernand raced so close together that, at Briançon, Michel looked worried for the first time. "Tomorrow the Galibier in the Alps. Though the incline of that pass isn't as steep as that of the Tourmalet in the Pyrenees, still, as you know, it's a long pull. And Fernand is powerful."

"I'm not afraid," André said.

"Don't be so cocky. You have to last now that Piaget is out. You've still got around five hundred miles to go before Paris. It's a crazy *Tour*, anyhow. A youngster like you carrying the Tricolores flag!"

"Let's talk it over with the Tricolores," said Jack. "It's got to be teamwork. I have a suggestion. Since I can't possibly win the *Tour* now, let me 'nurse' you, André, at the start tomorrow. I'll be your locomotive. I'll go ahead, and you ride in my wheel. That will save your strength, and you'll be all fresh for the attack in the Galibier, when I let you pass me and tear ahead."

It sounded so easy, but the next day, when Jack left him on his lonely climb, André thought he was never going to make it. He had gained three minutes on Fernand while riding "in Jack's wheel," but now he had the feeling that he was losing time. The people lining the road cheered him encouragingly. They all wanted so badly to give him a little push, but they knew too well that he would be penalized for it.

Now the Galibier was only six hundred yards away. André didn't dare to look behind him, but he felt in his bones and from the way the spectators acted that Fernand was not far behind. If only he could make that high point, marked by the monument to Henri Desgranges, the father of the *Tour*, then he would shoot down ahead.

Pedal, pedal. Each turn was painful; each turn a little

slower than the previous one. He strained and strained. Fatigue fell on him like a cloak of lead. On, on. His sight was blurred. He couldn't— And then suddenly, piercing the air, a baritone voice was singing,

> "The Sambre et Meuse Regiment
> Always answers liberty's call,
> Against us they were hundreds of thousands,
> And in command were kings."

Grandpa Isaac's voice! The old song rose, defiant and ardent, and gathered momentum and amplitude as people joined in and sang. It was just what André needed. All at once his tiredness was gone, his vision clear, his body taut. He dashed forward, reached the Galibier, and plunged down the other side, tearing after the Irish racer O'Toole.

O'Toole entered Aix-les-Bains first, but at last André took first place in the general score. Though this was good news, André could not feel elated yet. The fight with Fernand was so close that it was turning into a nightmare. Would André last? The least mishap now and he was done for. Indeed, he was still far from having won the *Tour*.

By this time all over France people were holding their breath during the twenty-four-hour rest before the time-trial race to Evian. Nobody had ever seen a *Tour* in which the champs were so young. Everybody said, "If Girard wins the time-trial race tomorrow he is made."

So when he did win, they shouted for joy at first; but they became more serious when they read Michel's column.

GIRARD WINS TIME-TRIAL RACE.

FINAL OUTCOME STILL UNPREDICTABLE.

In spite of a puncture which André Girard repaired in 50 seconds, the young Breton covered the 40 miles in 1 hour and 49 minutes.

The general score so far shows: Girard 113 hours, 17 minutes, 18 seconds. On the other hand, Fausset is only 3 minutes, 58 seconds, behind. The closeness of the score is frightening. It is evident that both racers will do their utmost from now on to win successive individual stretches in order to benefit from the time bonus given in such cases.

Next evening La Mouff' was full of excitement. The little café at Number 45 that had a radio was packed. People outside tried vainly to get information relayed to them. Someone said, "It's Renout."

Maman, who was on the sidewalk, asked, "Renout? What about him? And André, André Girard, what do they say?" But all she could hear was "Renout, Renout." Quickly she decided to go to the Monge subway station. Perhaps the evening papers had come.

Maman tore down the street. A pretty girl called, "Mrs. Girard, Mrs. Girard!" It was Miquette, her hand on her heart. They didn't have to say anything to each other. They just raced down. Hurry! Hurry!

They reached the subway station. The newspaper boy

bellowed, "Sensational! Sensational! Reversal in the *Tour!* Get your paper! Get your paper!"

Reversal? Maman's throat tightened. The last news was that Fernand was ahead on the road to Dijon. Suppose André had been hurt? People ran and pushed one another. Maman did the same. She reached the paper boy, flung some change at him, snatched up a still-wet sheet, and fought her way out of the crowd. Miquette got hold of a corner of the paper, and they both scanned the lines avidly. There it was, staring at them in big print: FAUSSET DISQUALIFIED.

"Hurray!" yelled Miquette, and she started doing a rumba right on the Boulevard St.-Germain. Maman was purple as she muttered, "And André? André?"

They found Michel's column.

Fausset had been ahead of Girard, who was himself closely followed by Renout, when suddenly, at Gevrey-Chambertin, Renout, taking advantage of the fact that he had been running in Girard's wheel, passed him and made a spectacular dash for Fausset.

As Renout got ahead of Fausset's wheel at the sprint at Dijon, Fausset stretched his elbow wide and gave Renout a tremendous push, which knocked him off his bike and sent him sprawling in the dust. Fausset passed the control tower victoriously, but of course he was instantly disqualified for the rest of the race.

Renout is thus the winner of the stretch, and Girard retains first place in the general score.

Both young racers received quite an ovation in the old capital of the Duke of Burgundy, but they retired early in order to tackle the last stretch, Dijon-Paris, tomorrow.

"He will make it!" said Miquette with shining eyes.

"Let's hope so!" whispered Maman.

"And to think that Jack beat Fernand too! Just as I always said, I want both André and Jack—"

"Don't forget," interrupted Maman, "that Jack made André's victory possible."

"True. But André himself is a great champ, the youngest champ there ever was! The— Ouch! Oh, my ear! Why, Papa, what are you doing here? And how do you do, Mr. Morel?"

"Yes, my daughter, André is a great champ. And I'm mighty pleased about our Jack too. Isn't it just as I always say—solidarity? That comes out plainly in this *Tour*, and for that wretched Fausset too. I tell you, I saw it coming years ago when the boys were still in school. I said Fernand would have to change his ways a lot if he wanted to race in the *Tour*."

"I know," said Miquette. "Mr. Valeur said so too. Jack told me at the time. I don't remember exactly, but it was about money and cheating not getting you anywhere in the long run."

"That's right, it catches up with you sooner or later. It's there for everybody to see in Michel's column every day."

"Ah," Maman said warmly, "how well Michel writes! He makes you feel you are right there. Not everybody can do that."

"Yes, I guess our Michel has writing talent," said Mr. Morel. "And I don't mean only technical ability. Our

Michel has feelings. He has a heart. It will be good to have him back tomorrow."

"I can't wait until tomorrow," said Miquette. "The arrival at the Parc des Princes. I hope André also wins the stretch itself."

"It doesn't matter now," said Mr. Renout. "Even if he doesn't, he's still far enough ahead in the general score now that Fausset is disqualified."

"Yes, he should make it," Mr. Morel said. "Yet, one never knows, one never knows."

"That's right," Mr. Renout said. "Anyway, no matter what happens now, Mrs. Girard, you can be proud of André."

"And you of Jack, Mr. Renout."

"And you of Michel, Mr. Morel."

"We can all be proud of the three of them, that's what I say!" Miquette announced.

"True!" they all chimed in as they shook hands. "See you tomorrow—at the Parc des Princes."

"They're coming! They're coming!"

All along the Dijon-Paris road, on the last hundred and fifty miles of the race, through the soft, rolling, smiling country, the phrase travels from one spectator to another.

On this beautiful Sunday in July, seventy-six racers shoot toward Paris. Twenty-one days ago, one hundred and fifteen of them made the start. The *Tour* took its yearly toll: casualties, collapses, eliminations, and disqualifications. Some who had to give up will try again, next year or later; some will succeed; some will abandon racing altogether.

The seventy-six who race toward Paris are this year's giants of the road, the "Modern Centaurs," as they are sometimes called. Through rain and shine, frost and fog, ups and downs; overcoming exhaustion, mishaps, and even treachery; by the sheer strength of their muscles and their will, and backed by years of severe training and by team cooperation, they have come to the finish of the most astounding annual sports event in the world.

As André looms ahead, the crowd's enthusiasm knows no bounds. *"Vive Dédé!* Hurray for Dédé!"

Vive Dédé!—what his buddies in the factory had shouted. Where are all of them now?

The police have a hard time keeping the people from spilling onto the road over and over again. This is the first time in the history of the *Tour* that a racer in his teens is winning. And he is French! The spectators cry themselves hoarse; the boys especially shout like mad and stamp their feet wildly.

Meanwhile, in the Parc des Princes Stadium in Paris forty thousand people are waiting. Such a beautiful sight! In the center is a green lawn, and all around it runs the delicate pink cement incline of the track. Around that, going up and up, is the huge strip of spectators, thousands of blue dots mostly, men's and boy's shirts, and here and there the red, pink, or yellow spot of a girl's blouse. And, above it all, a soft cloudless sky.

Mechanics, wearing dark blue jeans, stand ready by

the control tower, the *mirador,* from which the loudspeaker bellows the latest flashes. "They are at Monte-
reau. . . . They are at Melun . . ."

Between the announcements, in order to amuse the
spectators, different kinds of track races go on. At any
rate, the public cannot possibly be bored waiting. They
have too much to talk about: this year's race, the previous
years', racers past and present—all the legends and tales
of the *Tour de France.*

"Do you remember—"

Faber, who had to have twelve cooked lamb chops in
his feeding bag every day before starting?

Thys, who was the first racer ever to shave while racing?

Kubler, who attributed his victory to the fact that he
learned perseverance through gardening?

Speicher, the first racer to use a gear shift?

Lapebie, the vegetarian, who won five successive
stretches even though he had a large open wound in his
leg?

Frantz, who always shaved sitting down in order to save
his strength?

Zaaf, who drank a whole bottle of wine while racing
and later found himself *facing* the oncoming racers!

Magne, who in order to train his will compelled himself,
for years before he raced in the *Tour,* to move a heavy
rock in his garden first thing every single morning?

Christophe, the "Old Gaul," who repaired his broken
front fork himself on the anvil of a village blacksmith?

Pélissier, who nearly lost his life right in the Parc des

Princes when overenthusiastic spectators broke through the barriers and mobbed him?

Vietto the elevator boy? Meunier the telegraphist? Frantz the farmer? Lapize the office clerk? Trousselier the florist's apprentice? Bottechia the carpenter? Neffati of Tunisia, who was always cold? And some of the recent giants: handsome Bobet, Robic the Billy Goat, Koblet, who won the six-day race in New York?

And now André Girard.

"Did you know that he is the son of the great Girard who was injured before he could race in the *Tour?*"

"And I read in Mayer's column that his mother is a widow. His father was shot in the Resistance. So the boy had it hard. They were poor, and he went to work in a factory at the age of fourteen in order to buy himself a bicycle. From the time he could remember he had it on his mind to be a racer."

"He's a good-looking one too!"

"Listen to my wife! Ah, the women! Heard a girl say he's 'elegant.' "

"Well, he wasn't always. He was a sort of puny-looking duckling, they say. But he got himself in hand right from the start—even before he had his bike. He went in for self-discipline: no smoking, no drinking, plenty of fruit, early to bed, brisk walks, and so on. That's pluck for you!"

"You bet. And they say he's educated too. He speaks English, and he can hold his own in any conversation."

"Quite a guy! The bicycle-racer of the Atomic Age! Wonder what's going to happen to that other young chap,

Fausset, who was disqualified? He's a good racer, all right. It's tough. But he had it coming to him, no mistake!"

"They say he began to act mean way back when he was still a kid. He had it too easy. A rich uncle. He thought he could get away with it. Maybe this will teach him something. He's still young enough to learn."

"Maybe he will. In the *Tour,* money and cheating don't get you anywhere. You've got to deliver the goods, and that means training—*and* character."

"*And* solidarity. Don't forget, that's a big item too. The *Tour* is teamwork. Look at that Jack Renout and what he did."

"A swell guy, and a wonderful racer. Watch him next year!"

"Too bad about poor Piaget! It's hard luck!"

"He'll come back. He's not through yet by a long shot. He's still young."

"Daddy," asked a little boy, "how old are racers when they quit?"

"Usually around thirty-five."

"What do they do then?"

"They become managers of teams, or personal representatives of individual racers. Many open bicycle stores; others open restaurants for racers and their fans. Some buy small country places and just go there to live with their families and cultivate their gardens."

Now some of the former winners are here to take bows. Here is the very first winner of the *Tour,* way back in 1903, Maurice Garin. The small, elderly gentleman with a mustache and a flat cap makes a slow, dignified tour of the track on his bicycle, accompanied by a watchful young attendant, and gets a big ovation.

Here are Garrigou, Buysse, Coppi, Leduc, and many others, all champions, heroes, and lovers of the demanding, exacting, cruel, and magnificent *Tour*. Louison Bobet once said, "The *Tour*, it's an agony!" And they all know it—all those here today in the stadium, and the millions of fans in France who every year for twenty odd days give their unrestricted attention and heartfelt enthusiasm to the bicycle-racers.

The loudspeaker booms again. "They are detouring around Paris, in order to come in through the Versailles road directly into the stadium. André Girard leads."

A clamor of joy rises. Not only will André wear the Golden Fleece as the winner of the *Tour*, but he will be the first to enter Paris!

The loudspeaker continues, "The winner's prize is one million francs. Other prizes are as follows: the International Challenge Prize, awarded to the winning team; the prize to the best climber; the prize to the most aggressive; the prize to the racer who had the worst luck.

"All in all there are fifty million francs in prizes. The *Tour* itself costs one hundred and fifty million francs."

From Versailles to Paris the road is but one great cheer: Hurray for Dédé, hurray for Dédé! The crowd yells, shouts, shrieks, claps, jumps, weeps, and laughs. Cars blow their horns, motorcycles crack sharply, planes circle low. The noise is deafening. No king or queen or political figure has ever known such a popular, spontaneous, sweeping, triumphal welcome.

And in the midst of it all "Dédé" pedals and pedals. He hardly knows where he is or what he is doing. It is as if he had always pedaled, as if he could never stop pedaling, as if it had no beginning and would never end. He is not even conscious of the television cameraman who keeps up with him and films and films. It seems to him that he has been going in a circle on this bicycle ever since he was born.

Ahead there is a huge building in the midst of the trees. The traffic policemen point in one direction, toward the large tunnel which breaks through the building, the Parc des Princes Stadium, the end of the three-thousand-mile race, the closing of the Big Loop.

André is in, deafened by the noise of the gunshot, the thundering shouts and applause of the colorful sea of spectators, and wondering whether that bunch of people ahead of him there on the track is going to have sense enough to let him pass. He crosses the white line, and the mechanics carefully and firmly lay hold of him and his bicycle.

He steps down, and suddenly his exhausted body and his numbed mind rally, as he spots in the group of people surrounding him a pert little white cap with gay streamers, two elegant upturned white wings of starched linen, a short full skirt with a tight black velvet bodice, and a little hand-embroidered silk apron. Maman! Maman in her Breton costume! And all at once he knows: *he has won the Tour!*

Maman falls into his arms, and swiftly he lifts her up high for everybody to see. The crowd goes wild. "Bravo! Bravo! *Vive Dédé!*"

And now he sees them all around him: Miquette—so beautiful!—the twins, clapping like mad, the baby (a good size now) in Mr. Renout's arms, and Mrs. Renout, who keeps muttering, "White Rabbit, White Rabbit!" The Renout family. *Without Jack I couldn't have won.* Mr. and Mrs. Morel. *Michel's moral support meant everything to me.* And Grandpa Isaac. *Will I ever forget* Sambre et Meuse *and the Galibier?*

Here are all his buddies from the factory who gave him his start, including Pierre and the North African. They are bursting with pride. "Well done, Dédé, well done!" And here is old Valeur, so excited that he looks ten years younger. Because of him, André is not afraid of having to speak over the radio or of meeting the bigwigs later.

But who is that elderly couple who stays shyly behind? Mr. and Mrs. Williams! They have come all the way from Yellow Springs, Ohio! "Why not?"

André laughs. "Remember? My turn: champagne when I am a champ!" And he adds, making a circular gesture that includes the whole group, "Champagne for everybody afterward—Jack and Michel too. All together! Why not?"

Mr. Williams says, "We shall never forget it. There is nothing like it in the United States, or, I daresay, in the whole world."

And Mrs. Williams chimes in, "This is the wonderful France nobody back home knows anything about. We want to tell all about it in America."

Everybody in the group hugs and kisses André, and he kisses them all, men and women, on both cheeks, including Mr. and Mrs. Williams. He is covered with sweat and dirt. But who cares?

One attendant brings the winner's pullover and another brings a towel. André dries himself and then dons the Golden Fleece amidst continuous cheering. A huge spray of red gladiolas is handed to him. Cameras click; film turns; the microphone bellows, "Winner: André Girard in one hundred and twenty-nine hours, thirty-seven minutes, forty-three seconds. André Girard is the son of the great Girard, whom some of you may remember. Dédé, who is still in his teens, is the youngest racer ever to win the *Tour de France*."

People toot, shout, and clap. André stands smiling and a little awkward as he turns obligingly to this side and that for the photographers, who plead, "Look this way, Dédé!" "Please, Dédé, this way now!" "Let me take another one, Dédé!" "Just one more, please, Dédé!"

Once more André is on his bicycle, waving gaily at the delirious crowd, with the flowers in his arm for the track tour of honor.

Now the Tricolores, who have won the International Challenge Prize, are waiting for him by the control tower. Impetuously André goes up to Jack and holds him close, whispering quickly, "Without you—"

"You bet!" interrupts Jack, crossing his eyes in the funny way he used to do at school. "You bet it's got to be without me—your next move, that is. Did you see what's waiting for you outside?"

"What?"

"Writer's cramp: a truckload of pictures for you to autograph for all the schoolboys in France!"

"Watch out! Next year, *your* turn, Jack!"

They both laugh, and everybody cheers.

The Tricolores stand in a single line in front, each of them holding a big spray of pink gladiolas on their handlebars against their blue, white, and red pullovers. Jack is at the right of André, who is in the middle, wearing the Golden Fleece and carrying his red flowers. Each Tricolore puts his free arm around the shoulder of the one next to him and slowly makes a triumphal tour of the track.

When they come back, André is told that it is time for him to go to the official stand and receive his prize. Maman takes his arm and they go up together.

Here are the Minister of the Interior, the Minister of Public Works, the Senator from Finistère, Brittany— where Maman was born—the Deputy from Nantes, the Minister of Leisure, ambassadors from England, Italy, Holland, Belgium, the Representative of the Council of Europe, the French Ambassador to the United States, and many other important people.

And directly behind the official stand, going all the way to the upper seats, are hundreds of faces strangely familiar to André. Who are these people who are clapping and smiling as if they know him well? That's it! He has it! They are the people of Mouffetard Street. All La Mouff' is here! But these are expensive seats; how had they managed it? Ah, here is the Deputy for the Fifth District in Paris, which includes Mouffetard Street. That explains everything. Hurray for La Mouff'!

The band strikes up *La Marseillaise,* and everybody is on his feet. André feels that Maman, at his side, is ready to burst into tears. He tightens his grip around her and stands erect, looking far off.

There is a low whisper directly behind him. Michel's voice! "For all of us of the *Tour de France,* the real victory is the victory over ourselves."

Caen

Nantes

Bordeaux

Lourdes

Luchon

PAIN